The Armor of God

Christian fiction, Volume 11

Gregory Allen Parker

Published by Graywolf Press, 2024.

This is a work of fiction. Similarities to real people, places, or events are entirely coincidental.

THE ARMOR OF GOD

First edition. August 24, 2024.

Copyright © 2024 Gregory Allen Parker.

ISBN: 979-8224166312

Written by Gregory Allen Parker.

Table of Contents

To all the warriors of faith who battle in the unseen realms every day, standing firm in the truth of God's Word. This book is dedicated to you—may it strengthen your resolve, deepen your courage, and remind you that the victory is already won in Christ.

To my family and friends, whose prayers and encouragement have been my armor, I am deeply grateful. And above all, to the Lord Jesus Christ, our ultimate Warrior and King, who equips us with His armor and leads us in triumph—this work is for Your glory.

Chapter 1: The Belt of Truth

Theme: Understanding the foundation of truth in a Christian's life.

Reflection: Explore how truth is the foundation of spiritual warfare, binding everything together. Discuss the importance of living a life rooted in the truth of God's Word, and how this truth protects against the deception of the enemy.

In the vast array of spiritual armor described by the Apostle Paul in his letter to the Ephesians, the first piece mentioned is the belt of truth. At first glance, the belt might seem like an insignificant part of the armor, especially when compared to the more imposing elements like the breastplate or the sword. However, the belt plays a crucial role, and its significance in spiritual warfare is profound. In the context of a Christian's life, truth is not merely an accessory—it is the very foundation upon which everything else is built. Without truth, the rest of the armor would be ineffective, leaving the believer vulnerable to the enemy's attacks.

The Historical Context of the Belt

To fully appreciate the significance of the belt of truth, it is essential to understand its historical context. In Roman times, the belt, or "cingulum," was a vital part of a soldier's armor. It was not just a strip of leather worn around the waist; it was intricately designed to serve multiple purposes. The belt secured the soldier's tunic, preventing it from becoming a hindrance during battle. It also provided a place to hang the sword, keeping it within easy reach. Additionally, the belt was often adorned with small plates or studs, offering some degree of protection to the lower abdomen.

The belt was the first piece of armor a soldier would put on. Without it, the rest of the armor would be difficult to wear or even ineffective. The belt gathered and held everything together, allowing the soldier to move freely and confidently in battle. In this way, the belt of truth for the Christian serves a similar function—it holds together the spiritual armor and provides the foundation for everything else.

The Nature of Truth

Truth, in the biblical sense, is not just a set of facts or a collection of correct statements. It is far deeper and more profound. The Hebrew word for truth, "emet," carries the connotation of firmness, reliability, and faithfulness. It suggests something that is not only true in content but also trustworthy and steadfast. In the New Testament, the Greek word "aletheia" is used, which means uncovering or revealing the reality of something. Truth, then, is not just about being correct; it is about being real, genuine, and aligned with the very nature of God.

Jesus Himself declared, "I am the way, the truth, and the life" (John 14:6). In this profound statement, He identifies Himself as the embodiment of truth. For the Christian, truth is not an abstract concept but a person—Jesus Christ. To wear the belt of truth is to be wrapped in the reality of who Christ is and what He has done. It is to live in alignment with His teachings, His character, and His example.

Truth as the Foundation of Spiritual Warfare

In the context of spiritual warfare, truth is foundational because it defines the reality in which the battle takes place. The enemy, whom Jesus referred to as "the father of lies" (John 8:44), thrives in deception. His primary tactic is to distort, twist, and obscure the truth. He did this from the very beginning, when he questioned God's command to Adam and Eve, saying, "Did God really say...?" (Genesis 3:1). By sowing doubt and distorting the truth, the enemy led humanity into sin and separation from God.

Today, the enemy continues to use the same tactics. He attacks the truth of God's Word, the truth of who God is, and the truth of who we are in Christ. He seeks to undermine our confidence in God's promises and our identity as God's children. Without a firm grasp of the truth, we are vulnerable to these attacks. But when we are grounded in the truth, we can stand firm against the enemy's lies.

The Apostle Paul, in his letter to the Ephesians, urges believers to "stand firm then, with the belt of truth buckled around your waist" (Ephesians 6:14). This command emphasizes the importance of truth in maintaining a firm stance in spiritual warfare. Truth is not just a defensive measure; it is the ground upon which we stand. It is the reality that enables us to resist the enemy's deception and to walk in the freedom and authority that Christ has given us.

Living a Life Rooted in the Truth of God's Word

To wear the belt of truth is to live a life rooted in the truth of God's Word. The Bible is not just a collection of stories, moral teachings, or religious doctrines. It is the inspired, infallible, and authoritative Word of God. It is the ultimate standard of truth, revealing God's character, His will, and His plan for humanity. To live according to the truth of God's Word is to align our thoughts, words, and actions with His revealed will.

But living a life rooted in the truth of God's Word requires more than just intellectual assent. It requires a deep, personal commitment to studying, meditating on, and applying God's Word in our daily lives. The Psalmist declares, "Your word is a lamp for my feet, a light on my path" (Psalm 119:105). God's Word provides the guidance and direction we need to navigate the complexities of life. It illuminates the truth, exposing the lies and deceptions of the enemy.

However, living by the truth of God's Word is not always easy. We live in a world that often rejects absolute truth and embraces relativism, where truth is seen as subjective and personal rather than objective and universal. In such a cultural climate, holding fast to the truth of God's Word can be challenging. It may lead to opposition, persecution, and ridicule. But as Jesus prayed for His disciples, "Sanctify them by the truth; your word is truth" (John 17:17), we are reminded that it is through the truth of God's Word that we are set apart, sanctified, and made holy.

The Protection of Truth Against Deception

One of the primary functions of the belt of truth is to protect us against the deception of the enemy. Deception is a powerful weapon in the enemy's arsenal because it can lead us away from God, distort our understanding of reality, and cause us to make decisions that are contrary to God's will. Deception can take many forms—false teachings, half-truths, distorted interpretations of Scripture, or even lies about our own worth and identity.

The Apostle Paul warned the early church about the danger of deception, writing, "See to it that no one takes you captive through hollow and deceptive philosophy, which depends on human tradition and the elemental spiritual forces of this world rather than on Christ" (Colossians 2:8). Deception can lead us into captivity, enslaving us to ideas and beliefs that are contrary to the truth of God's Word.

But when we are girded with the belt of truth, we are equipped to discern and resist deception. The Holy Spirit, who is the "Spirit of truth" (John 16:13), guides us into all truth and helps us to recognize the lies of the enemy. He illuminates the Scriptures, giving us understanding and insight so that we can rightly divide the word of truth (2 Timothy 2:15). With the belt of truth securely fastened, we are able to stand firm, unmoved by the shifting winds of false doctrine and deceptive philosophies.

The Relationship Between Truth and Integrity

Truth is not just about what we believe; it is also about how we live. The belt of truth is closely linked to the concept of integrity. Integrity comes from the Latin word "integritas," which means wholeness, completeness, and soundness. A person of integrity is someone who is whole and undivided, whose actions are consistent with their beliefs. In other words, integrity is living in accordance with the truth.

The Apostle Paul exhorts believers to "live a life worthy of the calling you have received" (Ephesians 4:1). This means living a life of integrity, where our actions align with the truth of God's Word. When we wear the belt of truth, we are committed to living a life that reflects the truth we profess. This includes being honest in our dealings with others, being faithful to our commitments, and being consistent in our character.

Integrity is a powerful witness to the truth of the Gospel. When our lives are marked by integrity, we demonstrate the reality of God's truth to the world. Conversely, when we lack integrity, we undermine the message of the Gospel and give the enemy an opportunity to discredit our witness. The belt of truth, therefore, is not just about protecting ourselves from deception; it is also about ensuring that our lives are a testimony to the truth of God's Word.

Truth in the Midst of a Culture of Relativism

In our contemporary society, the concept of truth is often challenged by the prevailing culture of relativism. Relativism is the belief that truth is not absolute but is relative to individual perspectives, cultures, or situations. In a relativistic culture, what is true for one person may not be true for another, and truth becomes a matter of personal preference rather than objective reality.

This cultural shift has significant implications for how we understand and live out the truth of God's Word. The enemy uses relativism to undermine the authority of Scripture and to blur the lines between right and wrong, truth and falsehood. In such an environment, it is easy for Christians to become confused, compromised, or even indifferent to the truth.

However, the belt of truth calls us to stand firm in the conviction that truth is not relative but absolute. The truth of God's Word is unchanging and eternal, regardless of cultural trends or societal pressures. Jesus declared, "Heaven and earth will pass away, but my words will never pass away" (Matthew 24:35). The truth of God's Word is a solid foundation that we can rely on, even in the midst of a shifting cultural landscape.

Living by the belt of truth in a relativistic culture requires courage and discernment. It means being willing to stand for the truth, even when it is unpopular or countercultural. It also means being discerning in how we engage with the world, recognizing that not everything that is presented as truth aligns with the truth of God's Word. The belt of truth equips us to navigate these challenges with confidence and clarity.

The Transformative Power of Truth

Truth has a transformative power that goes beyond mere knowledge or understanding. When we embrace the truth of God's Word, it has the power to change us from the inside out. The Apostle Paul speaks of this transformative power in his letter to the Romans: "Do not conform to the pattern of this world, but be transformed by the renewing of your mind. Then you will be able to test and approve what God's will is—his good, pleasing and perfect will" (Romans 12:2).

The renewing of the mind is a process that involves aligning our thoughts, beliefs, and attitudes with the truth of God's Word. As we meditate on the truth and allow it to penetrate our hearts, it begins to shape our character, our desires, and our actions. The belt of truth, therefore, is not just a defensive piece of armor; it is also an agent of transformation that enables us to live in accordance with God's will.

The transformative power of truth is also evident in the process of sanctification. Sanctification is the ongoing work of the Holy Spirit in the life of a believer, making us more like Christ. Jesus prayed for His disciples, "Sanctify them by the truth; your word is truth" (John 17:17). It is through the truth of God's Word that we are sanctified, set apart, and made holy. The belt of truth plays a central role in this process, as it keeps us grounded in the reality of who God is and who we are in Him.

The Role of Community in Upholding the Truth

While the belt of truth is a personal piece of armor that each believer must put on, the pursuit of truth is not an individualistic endeavor. The Christian life is lived in community, and it is within the context of the church that we are called to uphold and live out the truth together. The Apostle Paul emphasizes the importance of community in the pursuit of truth when he writes, "Instead, speaking the truth in love, we will grow to become in every respect the mature body of him who is the head, that is, Christ" (Ephesians 4:15).

Speaking the truth in love is a key aspect of Christian community. It involves encouraging one another in the truth, holding one another accountable, and lovingly correcting one another when we stray from the truth. The belt of truth, therefore, is not just about individual protection; it is also about fostering a community that is committed to living by the truth.

The church, as the "pillar and foundation of the truth" (1 Timothy 3:15), has a responsibility to uphold and proclaim the truth of God's Word in a world that is often hostile to it. This involves not only teaching sound doctrine but also modeling lives that are consistent with the truth. When the church functions as a community of truth, it becomes a powerful witness to the world of the reality of God's kingdom.

Truth and the Battle for the Mind

The battlefield of spiritual warfare is often in the mind. The enemy knows that if he can control our thoughts, he can influence our actions. This is why the belt of truth is so crucial—it guards our minds against the lies and deceptions that the enemy seeks to implant. The Apostle Paul writes, "We demolish arguments and every pretension that sets itself up against the knowledge of God, and we take captive every thought to make it obedient to Christ" (2 Corinthians 10:5).

Taking every thought captive is a discipline that requires vigilance and discernment. It involves examining our thoughts in the light of God's Word and rejecting those that do not align with the truth. The belt of truth enables us to do this by providing the standard of truth against which all thoughts and ideas are measured.

The battle for the mind is not just about rejecting falsehood; it is also about filling our minds with the truth. The Apostle Paul exhorts believers, "Finally, brothers and sisters, whatever is true, whatever is noble, whatever is right, whatever is pure, whatever is lovely, whatever is admirable—if anything is excellent or praiseworthy—think about such things" (Philippians 4:8). By focusing our minds on the truth, we reinforce the belt of truth and strengthen our defense against the enemy's attacks.

The Belt of Truth in Everyday Life

While the belt of truth is often discussed in the context of spiritual warfare, it is also relevant to every aspect of our daily lives. Truth is not just something we put on when we are under attack; it is something we live by every day. The belt of truth shapes our relationships, our decisions, our work, and our worship. It affects how we interact with others, how we handle challenges, and how we pursue our goals.

In relationships, the belt of truth calls us to be honest, transparent, and trustworthy. It challenges us to speak the truth in love, to be faithful to our commitments, and to build relationships that are grounded in integrity. In our decisions, the belt of truth guides us to make choices that are in line with God's will, even when those choices are difficult or countercultural. In our work, the belt of truth reminds us to work with excellence, integrity, and a commitment to truthfulness, reflecting the character of Christ in all that we do.

In worship, the belt of truth calls us to worship God in spirit and in truth (John 4:24). It challenges us to be authentic in our worship, to offer God our whole selves, and to align our worship with the truth of who God is. The belt of truth ensures that our worship is not just an external act but a genuine expression of our love and devotion to God.

Conclusion: Girded with Truth

As we conclude this reflection on the belt of truth, it is important to remember that truth is not just an abstract concept or a set of beliefs. Truth is a person—Jesus Christ. To put on the belt of truth is to be wrapped in the reality of who Christ is and what He has done for us. It is to live in alignment with His teachings, His character, and His example.

The belt of truth is the foundation of our spiritual armor, holding everything together and enabling us to stand firm in the face of the enemy's attacks. It protects us against deception, guides us in the pursuit of integrity, and empowers us to live lives that reflect the truth of God's Word.

In a world that is often hostile to truth, the belt of truth equips us to stand firm, to resist the lies of the enemy, and to live lives that are a testimony to the reality of God's kingdom. As we gird ourselves with the belt of truth, let us commit to living lives that are rooted in the truth, transformed by the truth, and empowered by the truth. For it is the truth that sets us free (John 8:32), and it is the truth that enables us to stand firm in the victory that Christ has already won for us.

Chapter 2: The Breastplate of Righteousness

Theme: The significance of righteousness in protecting the heart.

Reflection: Reflect on the role of righteousness in guarding our hearts against the accusations and temptations of the enemy. Discuss how living a righteous life through Christ's righteousness shields us from spiritual harm.

In the spiritual battle that every believer faces, the heart is a critical target. It is the center of our emotions, desires, and intentions, and as such, it is vulnerable to attack from the enemy. The Apostle Paul, in his letter to the Ephesians, emphasizes the importance of guarding our hearts by wearing the breastplate of righteousness. This piece of spiritual armor is essential in protecting us from the assaults that the enemy launches against our inner being, particularly through accusations, temptations, and guilt. To fully understand the significance of the breastplate of righteousness, we must explore the nature of righteousness, the ways in which it protects us, and how we can live a life rooted in the righteousness of Christ.

The Historical and Biblical Context of the Breastplate

To appreciate the symbolism of the breastplate in spiritual warfare, it is helpful to understand its historical and biblical context. In the Roman military, the breastplate was a crucial piece of armor that covered the soldier's vital organs, particularly the heart and lungs. Made of bronze or iron, the breastplate was designed to deflect arrows, swords, and other weapons that could penetrate the body and cause fatal injuries. Without a breastplate, a soldier was extremely vulnerable in battle, as even a minor wound to the chest could be deadly.

In the Old Testament, the breastplate also appears as a significant piece of the high priest's attire. Known as the breastplate of judgment, it was worn over the ephod and was embedded with twelve precious stones, each representing one of the twelve tribes of Israel (Exodus 28:15-21). The high priest wore this breastplate when he entered the Holy of Holies to make atonement for the sins of the people. The breastplate symbolized the righteousness and justice of

God, reminding the people of Israel of their need for divine protection and atonement.

When Paul instructs believers to put on the breastplate of righteousness, he draws on these rich traditions to convey a powerful spiritual truth. Just as the Roman soldier's breastplate protected his heart from physical attacks, and the high priest's breastplate represented the righteousness of God in atoning for sin, the breastplate of righteousness in spiritual warfare protects the believer's heart from spiritual harm. It is a defense against the enemy's attempts to wound, corrupt, or deceive our hearts, ensuring that we remain steadfast and pure in our walk with God.

The Nature of Righteousness

To understand the role of the breastplate of righteousness, we must first examine the nature of righteousness itself. In both the Old and New Testaments, righteousness is a central theme, closely associated with God's character and His relationship with humanity. The Hebrew word for righteousness, "tzedek," and the Greek word "dikaiosyne" both carry the connotation of justice, fairness, and moral integrity. Righteousness is not merely about following a set of rules or adhering to a moral code; it is about living in right relationship with God and with others.

In the Old Testament, righteousness is often associated with covenant faithfulness. God is described as righteous because He is faithful to His covenant promises, acting in accordance with His character and His word. For humans, righteousness involves living in accordance with God's laws and maintaining a faithful relationship with Him. The psalmist declares, "The Lord is righteous in all his ways and faithful in all he does" (Psalm 145:17), emphasizing that God's righteousness is inseparable from His faithfulness.

In the New Testament, the concept of righteousness takes on a deeper, more personal dimension. Through the life, death, and resurrection of Jesus Christ, God's righteousness is revealed in a way that goes beyond the law. Paul writes, "But now apart from the law the righteousness of God has been made known, to which the Law and the Prophets testify. This righteousness is given through faith in Jesus Christ to all who believe" (Romans 3:21-22). In Christ, righteousness is no longer about our ability to keep the law, but about our relationship with Him. We are declared righteous, not because of our works, but because of our faith in Christ and His atoning sacrifice.

This righteousness is both imputed and imparted. Imputed righteousness means that when we place our faith in Christ, His righteousness is credited to us. God no longer sees our sin; instead, He sees the righteousness of His Son. Paul explains, "God made him who had no sin to be sin for us, so that in him we might become the righteousness of God" (2 Corinthians 5:21). This is a profound mystery of the gospel—that through Christ, we are declared righteous before God, not because of anything we have done, but because of what Christ has done for us.

Imparted righteousness, on the other hand, refers to the ongoing work of the Holy Spirit in our lives, transforming us into the likeness of Christ. As we grow in our relationship with God, the righteousness of Christ begins to shape our thoughts, attitudes, and actions. This process, known as sanctification, is a lifelong journey of becoming more like Christ in our daily lives. Paul writes, "For those God foreknew he also predestined to be conformed to the image of his Son" (Romans 8:29). Through the power of the Holy Spirit, we are continually being transformed into the image of Christ, living out His righteousness in our lives.

Righteousness as a Defense Against Accusations

One of the primary functions of the breastplate of righteousness is to protect us against the accusations of the enemy. The Bible describes Satan as the "accuser of the brethren" (Revelation 12:10), who constantly seeks to undermine our confidence in God's love and forgiveness by reminding us of our sins and failures. These accusations can be powerful weapons in spiritual warfare, as they can lead us to doubt our salvation, feel unworthy of God's love, and become paralyzed by guilt and shame.

However, the breastplate of righteousness provides a defense against these accusations. When we wear this breastplate, we are reminded that our righteousness is not based on our own works, but on the finished work of Christ. His righteousness is perfect, complete, and unassailable. No accusation can penetrate the righteousness of Christ that covers us. Paul writes, "Who will bring any charge against those whom God has chosen? It is God who justifies.

Who then is the one who condemns? No one. Christ Jesus who died—more than that, who was raised to life—is at the right hand of God and is also interceding for us" (Romans 8:33-34).

When we are clothed in the righteousness of Christ, we can stand confidently before God, knowing that we are fully justified, fully forgiven, and fully accepted. The enemy's accusations may come, but they have no power over us because we are covered by the righteousness of Christ. The breastplate of righteousness, therefore, is not just a defense against external attacks; it is a source of inner peace and assurance, reminding us of our secure position in Christ.

Righteousness as a Defense Against Temptations

In addition to protecting us from accusations, the breastplate of righteousness also guards our hearts against the temptations of the enemy. Temptation is a reality that every believer faces, and it often targets the desires and inclinations of our hearts. The enemy seeks to lure us away from God by appealing to our fleshly desires, offering us shortcuts to satisfaction, happiness, or success. However, these temptations are ultimately deceptive, leading to spiritual harm and separation from God.

The breastplate of righteousness helps us to resist temptation by reminding us of our identity in Christ and the righteousness we have received through Him. When we understand that we are already made righteous in Christ, we are less likely to seek fulfillment in sinful pursuits. The righteousness of Christ becomes our protection against the lies and allurements of the enemy, enabling us to stand firm in the face of temptation.

Paul encourages believers to "put on the new self, created to be like God in true righteousness and holiness" (Ephesians 4:24). This new self is our identity in Christ—a new creation that reflects His righteousness and holiness. When we embrace this identity, we are empowered to live in a way that is consistent with our new nature. The breastplate of righteousness, therefore, is not just about resisting temptation; it is about living out the righteousness that we have received in Christ, making choices that align with our identity as children of God.

Moreover, the breastplate of righteousness enables us to discern between the true and the false, the holy and the unholy. Temptation often comes in subtle forms, presenting sin as something desirable or harmless. But when we are girded with the breastplate of righteousness, we have the discernment to recognize the enemy's lies and the strength to resist them. The Psalmist declares, "I have hidden your word in my heart that I might not sin against you" (Psalm 119:11). The Word of God, which reveals His righteousness, becomes our guide and our protection against the deceptive tactics of the enemy.

Righteousness and the Pursuit of Holiness

The breastplate of righteousness not only protects us from accusations and temptations but also calls us to a life of holiness. Holiness is the outworking of righteousness in our daily lives—it is the practical expression of our righteous standing before God. The Bible repeatedly calls believers to be holy, as God is holy (1 Peter 1:15-16). This call to holiness is not about legalism or self-righteousness, but about living in a way that reflects the character of God and honors His name.

Holiness involves a separation from sin and a dedication to God. It is about setting our hearts and minds on things above, not on earthly things (Colossians 3:2). The breastplate of righteousness helps us in this pursuit by protecting our hearts from the corruption of sin and keeping us focused on our calling to live a holy life. As we grow in holiness, we become more attuned to the will of God, more sensitive to the leading of the Holy Spirit, and more effective in our witness to the world.

Living a life of holiness also involves the cultivation of godly virtues. Paul writes, "Put on the new self, which is being renewed in knowledge in the image of its Creator" (Colossians 3:10). As we put on the breastplate of righteousness, we are called to put off the old self, with its sinful desires and behaviors, and to put on the new self, which reflects the image of Christ. This involves a daily commitment to growing in virtues such as love, patience, kindness, humility, and self-control (Galatians 5:22-23). These virtues are the fruit of righteousness, and they serve as a testimony to the transforming power of Christ in our lives.

Righteousness and the Heart

The heart is central to the concept of righteousness in the Bible. In biblical thought, the heart is not just the seat of emotions, but the core of a person's being—the center of their thoughts, desires, and intentions. The condition of the heart is of utmost importance to God, as it determines the course of a person's life. The book of Proverbs warns, "Above all else, guard your heart, for everything you do flows from it" (Proverbs 4:23).

Righteousness, therefore, is not just about external behavior; it is about the condition of the heart. Jesus emphasized this when He said, "Blessed are the pure in heart, for they will see God" (Matthew 5:8). A pure heart is one that is free from sin, hypocrisy, and double-mindedness. It is a heart that is fully devoted to God, seeking His will above all else. The breastplate of righteousness protects the heart by covering it with the righteousness of Christ, ensuring that our hearts remain pure and undefiled by sin.

However, the heart is also the target of the enemy's attacks. The enemy knows that if he can corrupt our hearts, he can lead us away from God and into sin. This is why the breastplate of righteousness is so crucial—it guards our hearts against the enemy's attempts to sow seeds of bitterness, envy, lust, pride, and other sinful desires. The Psalmist prays, "Create in me a pure heart, O God, and renew a steadfast spirit within me" (Psalm 51:10). This prayer reflects the ongoing need for God's righteousness to cleanse and protect our hearts.

Living a Righteous Life Through Christ's Righteousness

As we reflect on the significance of the breastplate of righteousness, it is important to recognize that living a righteous life is not something we can achieve on our own. Righteousness is a gift from God, given to us through faith in Christ. It is through His righteousness that we are justified, sanctified, and ultimately glorified. Paul writes, "For it is by grace you have been saved, through faith—and this is not from yourselves, it is the gift of God—not by works, so that no one can boast" (Ephesians 2:8-9).

Living a righteous life, therefore, begins with recognizing our dependence on Christ and His grace. It involves surrendering our own efforts to earn righteousness and embracing the righteousness that comes from God. This is a humbling process, as it requires us to acknowledge our own sinfulness and our need for a Savior. But it is also a liberating process, as it frees us from the burden of trying to earn God's favor through our own works.

Once we have received the righteousness of Christ, we are called to live out that righteousness in our daily lives. This involves a continual reliance on the Holy Spirit, who empowers us to live in a way that honors God. The breastplate of righteousness is not just about protecting us from the enemy's attacks; it is also about enabling us to live a life that reflects the character of Christ. Paul writes, "For in the gospel the righteousness of God is revealed—a righteousness that is by faith from first to last, just as it is written: 'The righteous will live by faith'" (Romans 1:17).

Living by faith means trusting in God's promises, following His leading, and obeying His commands, even when it is difficult or costly. It means walking in the Spirit, rather than in the flesh, and allowing the righteousness of Christ to guide our thoughts, words, and actions. As we live by faith, we experience the protection and peace that come from wearing the breastplate of righteousness.

The Peace and Confidence of Righteousness

One of the fruits of living a righteous life through Christ's righteousness is the peace and confidence that it brings. When we are clothed in the righteousness of Christ, we can approach God with boldness and assurance, knowing that we are fully accepted and loved by Him. This confidence is not based on our own merit, but on the finished work of Christ. The writer of Hebrews encourages believers, "Let us then approach God's throne of grace with confidence, so that we may receive mercy and find grace to help us in our time of need" (Hebrews 4:16).

This confidence extends beyond our relationship with God to every area of our lives. When we are secure in our identity as righteous in Christ, we are less likely to be swayed by the opinions of others, intimidated by the challenges we face, or discouraged by our own failures. The breastplate of righteousness gives us the confidence to stand firm in the face of adversity, knowing that we are protected by the righteousness of Christ.

Furthermore, the peace that comes from righteousness is a deep, abiding peace that transcends circumstances. It is the peace that Paul describes in Philippians 4:7 as "the peace of God, which transcends all understanding." This peace guards our hearts and minds, even in the midst of trials and tribulations. It is a peace that is rooted in the knowledge that we are reconciled to God through Christ, and that nothing can separate us from His love.

The Role of the Church in Upholding Righteousness

While the breastplate of righteousness is a personal piece of spiritual armor, the pursuit of righteousness is not an individualistic endeavor. The church, as the body of Christ, plays a crucial role in upholding and promoting righteousness among its members. Paul writes, "Let us consider how we may spur one another on toward love and good deeds" (Hebrews 10:24). The church is called to be a community where righteousness is encouraged, nurtured, and celebrated.

This involves both teaching and modeling righteousness. The church is responsible for proclaiming the truth of the gospel, which reveals the righteousness of God and calls people to live in accordance with it. This includes teaching sound doctrine, correcting false teachings, and providing guidance on how to live a righteous life. The church is also responsible for modeling righteousness through the lives of its leaders and members, demonstrating what it means to live in a way that honors God.

Furthermore, the church provides a supportive community where believers can hold one another accountable and encourage one another in the pursuit of righteousness. This accountability is crucial, as it helps us to stay on the path of righteousness and to resist the temptations and pressures of the world. Paul writes, "Brothers and sisters, if someone is caught in a sin, you who live by the Spirit should restore that person gently. But watch yourselves, or you also may be tempted" (Galatians 6:1). The church is called to be a place of restoration and healing, where believers can grow in righteousness together.

Conclusion: Clothed in the Righteousness of Christ

As we conclude this reflection on the breastplate of righteousness, it is important to remember that righteousness is not something we achieve through our own efforts, but something we receive through faith in Christ. The breastplate of righteousness is a gift from God, given to us to protect our hearts and to empower us to live a life that honors Him.

When we wear the breastplate of righteousness, we are clothed in the righteousness of Christ. This righteousness protects us from the accusations and temptations of the enemy, enables us to pursue holiness, and gives us the peace and confidence that come from knowing we are fully accepted by God. The breastplate of righteousness is not just a piece of armor; it is a way of life—a life that reflects the character of Christ and brings glory to God.

As we go forth into the battles of life, let us remember to put on the breastplate of righteousness, trusting in the righteousness of Christ to guard our hearts and guide our steps. Let us live in the confidence that comes from being clothed in His righteousness, and let us pursue a life of holiness that reflects the beauty and majesty of our Savior. For it is through His righteousness that we are made whole, and it is through His righteousness that we will stand firm in the day of battle.

Chapter 3: The Shoes of the Gospel of Peace

Theme: The readiness and stability that comes from the Gospel.

Reflection: Examine how the Gospel of peace prepares us to stand firm against the enemy's attacks. Reflect on the peace that comes from knowing the Gospel and how it provides stability in the midst of spiritual battles.

In the spiritual armor that the Apostle Paul describes in his letter to the Ephesians, one of the most critical yet often overlooked pieces is the shoes, or as Paul describes them, "having shod your feet with the preparation of the gospel of peace" (Ephesians 6:15). The shoes of the gospel of peace symbolize the readiness and stability that the Gospel provides to believers. In the context of spiritual warfare, these shoes are not merely about protection; they are about mobility, preparedness, and standing firm. They represent the grounding of our lives in the peace that comes from the Gospel, enabling us to navigate the challenges of life with confidence and poise.

The Historical Context of the Soldier's Shoes

To fully grasp the significance of the shoes in the armor of God, it is helpful to consider the historical context of a Roman soldier's footwear. The shoes, or "caligae," worn by Roman soldiers were not ordinary sandals. They were specially designed for battle, constructed with thick soles and studded with nails or spikes, providing both protection and stability. These shoes allowed soldiers to march long distances without injury and to stand firm in combat, even on uneven or slippery terrain. The spikes on the soles ensured that the soldiers would not easily lose their footing, giving them an advantage in battle.

Without proper footwear, a soldier would be vulnerable to injury and would struggle to maintain their position in the heat of battle. Just as the caligae were essential for the physical readiness of a Roman soldier, the shoes of the gospel of peace are essential for the spiritual readiness of a Christian. They prepare us to stand firm in the face of the enemy's attacks and to move forward with confidence, grounded in the truth and peace of the Gospel.

The Gospel of Peace: A Foundation for Readiness

At the heart of the shoes of the gospel of peace is the concept of readiness. Readiness, in this context, refers to being prepared, equipped, and poised for action. The Gospel of peace provides this readiness by grounding us in the truth of who God is, what He has done for us through Christ, and what our standing is before Him. This foundational understanding gives us the stability and confidence we need to face spiritual battles.

The Gospel, or "good news," is the message of Jesus Christ—His life, death, and resurrection for the forgiveness of sins and the reconciliation of humanity with God. This message is central to the Christian faith and is the source of our peace. Paul writes in Romans, "Therefore, since we have been justified through faith, we have peace with God through our Lord Jesus Christ" (Romans 5:1). This peace is not merely a subjective feeling; it is an objective reality, a state of being that comes from our restored relationship with God. Through the Gospel, we are no longer enemies of God, but His children, reconciled and at peace with Him.

This peace with God provides the foundation for our readiness in spiritual warfare. It gives us the confidence to stand firm, knowing that we are secure in our relationship with God and that nothing can separate us from His love (Romans 8:38-39). It also gives us the assurance that, regardless of the circumstances we face, we are in God's hands, and He is working all things together for our good (Romans 8:28). This readiness is not about self-confidence or self-reliance; it is about being grounded in the unshakable truth of the Gospel and the peace that it brings.

The Peace of the Gospel in the Midst of Spiritual Battles

One of the most profound aspects of the Gospel is the peace it brings, not only in our relationship with God but also in our daily lives, especially in the midst of spiritual battles. Spiritual warfare is a reality for every believer, and the enemy often seeks to disrupt our peace through fear, anxiety, confusion, and doubt. However, the Gospel of peace provides a stabilizing force that enables us to remain calm, focused, and steadfast, even in the face of intense opposition.

Jesus Himself spoke of this peace when He said, "Peace I leave with you; my peace I give you. I do not give to you as the world gives. Do not let your hearts be troubled and do not be afraid" (John 14:27). The peace that Jesus offers is different from the peace that the world offers. It is not dependent on external circumstances but is rooted in the unchanging reality of His presence and His promises. This peace guards our hearts and minds, enabling us to face the trials of life without being overwhelmed by fear or anxiety.

In spiritual warfare, the enemy often tries to rob us of this peace by sowing seeds of doubt and fear. He whispers lies that make us question God's goodness, His faithfulness, and His love for us. He brings up our past failures and sins, trying to convince us that we are unworthy of God's peace. He creates confusion and chaos, attempting to destabilize us and cause us to lose our footing.

But when we are grounded in the Gospel of peace, we can resist these attacks. The peace of the Gospel acts as an anchor for our souls, keeping us steady and secure, even in the midst of the storm. Paul writes in Philippians, "And the peace of God, which transcends all understanding, will guard your hearts and your minds in Christ Jesus" (Philippians 4:7). This peace is a supernatural gift from God that goes beyond human comprehension. It is a peace that remains even when circumstances are difficult, and it guards our hearts and minds against the enemy's attacks.

The Role of Peace in Stability and Firmness

The shoes of the gospel of peace not only provide readiness but also stability. In the context of spiritual warfare, stability is the ability to stand firm, to hold one's ground, and to remain unshaken by the enemy's attacks. This stability comes from being firmly rooted in the peace of the Gospel.

Paul frequently emphasizes the importance of standing firm in the faith. He writes to the Corinthians, "Be on your guard; stand firm in the faith; be courageous; be strong" (1 Corinthians 16:13). To the Philippians, he exhorts, "Stand firm in the Lord in this way, dear friends!" (Philippians 4:1). Standing firm is a recurring theme in Paul's writings because he understands that spiritual warfare requires a steadfast and unyielding stance. The enemy will try to push us off balance, to make us stumble, and to cause us to waver in our faith. But when we are grounded in the peace of the Gospel, we can stand firm, knowing that our foundation is secure.

The stability that comes from the Gospel of peace is not about physical strength or mental fortitude; it is about spiritual grounding. It is about being rooted in the truth of the Gospel and allowing that truth to permeate every area of our lives. When we are stable in our faith, we are less likely to be swayed by the opinions of others, the pressures of the world, or the lies of the enemy. We are able to discern truth from falsehood, to hold fast to our convictions, and to remain faithful to God's calling, even when it is difficult.

This stability is also evident in the way we respond to life's challenges. When we are grounded in the Gospel of peace, we are not easily shaken by trials or tribulations. We are able to face difficulties with a sense of calm and assurance, knowing that our peace does not come from our circumstances but from our relationship with God. This stability allows us to be resilient, to persevere through adversity, and to maintain our trust in God, even when the road is tough.

The Readiness to Proclaim the Gospel

The shoes of the gospel of peace not only prepare us to stand firm but also equip us to move forward with the mission of proclaiming the Gospel. Just as a soldier's shoes enable him to march into battle, the shoes of the gospel of peace enable us to advance the kingdom of God by sharing the good news with others.

The Gospel of peace is not just for our personal benefit; it is a message that we are called to share with the world. Jesus commissioned His disciples to "go and make disciples of all nations" (Matthew 28:19), and this commission extends to every believer. The shoes of the gospel of peace represent our readiness to take the Gospel to others, to spread the message of God's love, grace, and peace to those who are lost and in need of salvation.

This readiness to proclaim the Gospel requires both boldness and sensitivity. It requires boldness because sharing the Gospel often involves stepping out of our comfort zones, facing rejection or opposition, and standing up for our faith in a world that is often hostile to it. But it also requires sensitivity because the Gospel is a message of peace, and we are called to share it in a way that reflects the love and compassion of Christ.

Paul writes in Romans, "How, then, can they call on the one they have not believed in? And how can they believe in the one of whom they have not heard? And how can they hear without someone preaching to them? And how can anyone preach unless they are sent? As it is written: 'How beautiful are the feet of those who bring good news!'" (Romans 10:14-15). The readiness to proclaim the Gospel is a beautiful thing in the eyes of God because it is through the proclamation of the Gospel that people come to know Him and experience His peace.

The Transformative Power of the Gospel of Peace

The Gospel of peace is not just a message; it is a transformative power that changes lives. When we accept the Gospel, we are not only reconciled to God, but we are also transformed by His peace. This peace begins to permeate every area of our lives, bringing healing, restoration, and wholeness.

In Ephesians, Paul describes the transformative power of the Gospel by saying, "He came and preached peace to you who were far away and peace to those who were near. For through him we both have access to the Father by one Spirit" (Ephesians 2:17-18). The peace that Christ brings is a reconciling peace—it breaks down the barriers of sin and separation and unites us with God and with one another. This peace transforms our relationships, our attitudes, and our actions.

The transformative power of the Gospel of peace is also evident in the way it changes our perspective on life. When we are grounded in the peace of the Gospel, we begin to see the world through the lens of God's love and grace. We become more compassionate, more forgiving, and more patient with others. We become peacemakers, seeking to bring reconciliation and healing to broken relationships. Jesus said, "Blessed are the peacemakers, for they will be called children of God" (Matthew 5:9). As we live out the Gospel of peace, we reflect the character of God and become agents of His peace in the world.

The Peace of the Gospel in the Face of Persecution

The shoes of the gospel of peace are particularly significant in the context of persecution. Throughout history, Christians have faced persecution for their faith, and many continue to do so today. In the face of persecution, the peace of the Gospel provides the strength and courage to stand firm, even when it comes at a great cost.

Jesus warned His disciples that they would face persecution, saying, "If the world hates you, keep in mind that it hated me first. If you belonged to the world, it would love you as its own. As it is, you do not belong to the world, but I have chosen you out of the world. That is why the world hates you" (John 15:18-19). Persecution is a reality for those who follow Christ, but the peace of the Gospel equips us to endure it with grace and perseverance.

In the early church, the peace of the Gospel was a source of strength for believers who faced imprisonment, torture, and death for their faith. Despite the intense suffering they endured, they remained steadfast in their commitment to Christ, often going to their deaths with a sense of peace and even joy. This peace was not the absence of fear, but the presence of Christ in the midst of their trials.

The same peace is available to us today. When we face persecution, whether it is in the form of ridicule, discrimination, or more severe forms of suffering, the peace of the Gospel enables us to remain faithful to Christ. It reminds us that our hope is not in this world, but in the eternal kingdom of God. It gives us the courage to stand firm, to forgive those who persecute us, and to continue to proclaim the Gospel, even in the face of opposition.

The Role of Faith in Maintaining Peace

While the Gospel of peace provides the foundation for our readiness and stability, it is our faith that enables us to maintain this peace in the midst of spiritual battles. Faith is the means by which we appropriate the promises of God and stand firm in the truth of the Gospel.

The Bible teaches that faith is essential for experiencing the peace of God. Paul writes, "Therefore, since we have been justified through faith, we have peace with God through our Lord Jesus Christ" (Romans 5:1). It is through faith that we are justified, and it is through faith that we experience the peace that comes from being reconciled to God. Without faith, we cannot experience the fullness of the peace that the Gospel offers.

Faith also plays a crucial role in maintaining our peace when we face challenges and trials. The enemy often attacks our faith by sowing seeds of doubt and unbelief, trying to undermine our trust in God and His promises. But when we stand firm in our faith, we are able to resist these attacks and maintain our peace. Paul encourages believers to "take up the shield of faith, with which you can extinguish all the flaming arrows of the evil one" (Ephesians 6:16). The shield of faith protects us from the enemy's attacks and enables us to stand firm in the peace of the Gospel.

Furthermore, faith enables us to trust in God's sovereignty and goodness, even when we do not understand our circumstances. It allows us to rest in the knowledge that God is in control and that He is working all things together for our good (Romans 8:28). This trust in God's character and His promises is the foundation of our peace, and it is what enables us to remain steadfast, even in the face of uncertainty and difficulty.

The Peace of the Gospel in Everyday Life

The peace of the Gospel is not just for times of spiritual warfare or persecution; it is also for everyday life. The shoes of the gospel of peace equip us to navigate the challenges, stresses, and uncertainties of daily life with a sense of calm and assurance.

In our relationships, the peace of the Gospel enables us to live at peace with others, even when conflicts arise. Paul writes, "If it is possible, as far as it depends on you, live at peace with everyone" (Romans 12:18). The Gospel of peace calls us to be peacemakers, to seek reconciliation, and to forgive those who have wronged us. It empowers us to let go of grudges, to extend grace, and to build bridges rather than walls.

In our work, the peace of the Gospel gives us the strength to handle the pressures and demands of our jobs without being overwhelmed by stress or anxiety. It reminds us that our identity is not in our work, but in Christ, and that our ultimate security is in Him, not in our career or financial success. This peace enables us to work diligently and faithfully, without being consumed by worry or fear.

In our personal lives, the peace of the Gospel helps us to deal with the uncertainties and challenges that we face, whether it is health issues, financial struggles, or family concerns. The peace of the Gospel reminds us that God is with us, that He cares for us, and that He will provide for our needs. It gives us the confidence to face each day with hope and trust, knowing that we are in God's hands.

The Eternal Peace of the Gospel

The peace that the Gospel brings is not just for this life; it is an eternal peace that will be fully realized in the kingdom of God. The Bible speaks of a future time when God will establish His kingdom in its fullness, and there will be perfect peace—shalom—in all creation. This is the ultimate hope of the Gospel, and it is a source of great comfort and assurance for believers.

In the book of Revelation, John describes a vision of this future peace: "He will wipe every tear from their eyes. There will be no more death or mourning or crying or pain, for the old order of things has passed away" (Revelation 21:4). This is the peace that we long for, a peace that will be fully realized when Christ returns and establishes His kingdom. Until that day, we experience glimpses of this peace through the Gospel, but we look forward to the day when it will be fully and perfectly realized.

The eternal peace of the Gospel gives us the perspective we need to endure the challenges of this life. It reminds us that our present sufferings are temporary and that they are not worth comparing with the glory that will be revealed in us (Romans 8:18). It gives us the hope and the strength to persevere, knowing that our future is secure in Christ and that we will one day experience the fullness of His peace.

Conclusion: Walking in the Shoes of the Gospel of Peace

As we conclude this reflection on the shoes of the gospel of peace, it is important to recognize that these shoes are not just a metaphorical piece of armor; they are a way of life. Walking in the shoes of the gospel of peace means living each day grounded in the truth and peace of the Gospel, ready to stand firm in the face of spiritual battles, and prepared to advance the kingdom of God by sharing the good news with others.

The peace of the Gospel provides the readiness and stability we need to navigate the challenges of life with confidence and assurance. It equips us to stand firm against the enemy's attacks, to remain calm in the midst of trials, and to move forward with the mission of proclaiming the Gospel. It is a peace that transcends circumstances, a peace that guards our hearts and minds, and a peace that points us to the hope of eternal peace in the kingdom of God.

As we go forth into the battles of life, let us remember to put on the shoes of the gospel of peace, trusting in the peace that comes from knowing Christ and His finished work on the cross. Let us live each day in the readiness and stability that the Gospel provides, and let us be agents of His peace in a world that desperately needs it. For it is the peace of the Gospel that will sustain us, guide us, and ultimately lead us to the fullness of life in Christ.

Chapter 4: The Shield of Faith

Theme: Faith as a defense against spiritual attacks.

Reflection: Delve into the protective power of faith, which can extinguish all the flaming arrows of the evil one. Reflect on how faith in God's promises and His character is crucial in deflecting doubt, fear, and lies from the enemy.

In the ancient world, a shield was one of the most critical pieces of a soldier's armor. It was a versatile and essential tool for defense, designed to protect the warrior from the enemy's attacks. In his letter to the Ephesians, the Apostle Paul uses the metaphor of a shield to describe faith, emphasizing its importance in the spiritual armor of a Christian. He writes, "In addition to all this, take up the shield of faith, with which you can extinguish all the flaming arrows of the evil one" (Ephesians 6:16). In this chapter, we will explore the significance of faith as a shield, examining how it protects us from spiritual attacks and why it is essential in our walk with God.

The Historical Context of the Roman Shield

To fully appreciate the metaphor of the shield of faith, it is helpful to understand the historical context of the Roman shield, or "scutum." The scutum was a large, rectangular shield made of wood, covered with leather, and reinforced with metal. It was designed to protect the soldier's entire body, allowing him to withstand both direct and indirect attacks. The shield was not only a defensive tool but also an offensive one, as it could be used to push back against the enemy, creating space for a counterattack.

One of the most notable features of the Roman shield was its ability to interlock with the shields of other soldiers, forming a protective barrier known as the "testudo" or "tortoise" formation. This formation provided a nearly impenetrable defense, allowing soldiers to advance or hold their position while being protected from enemy fire. The shield was often soaked in water before battle to extinguish flaming arrows shot by the enemy, a tactic that Paul directly references when he speaks of the shield of faith extinguishing the flaming arrows of the evil one.

The shield was not an optional piece of equipment for a Roman soldier; it was essential for survival in battle. Similarly, faith is not an optional part of the Christian life; it is vital for withstanding the attacks of the enemy. Just as a soldier would never enter the battlefield without his shield, a Christian should never face spiritual warfare without the shield of faith.

The Nature of Faith as a Shield

Faith, in the biblical sense, is more than mere belief or intellectual assent; it is a deep trust and confidence in God—His character, His promises, and His power. The Greek word for faith, "pistis," carries the connotation of trust, reliance, and steadfastness. Faith is the means by which we hold onto God's promises, even when we cannot see their fulfillment. It is the assurance of things hoped for and the conviction of things not seen (Hebrews 11:1).

As a shield, faith functions in several ways. First, it serves as a protective barrier against the attacks of the enemy. The enemy, whom the Bible describes as a roaring lion seeking to devour (1 Peter 5:8), constantly launches spiritual attacks against believers. These attacks often come in the form of doubts, fears, lies, temptations, and accusations. The purpose of these attacks is to undermine our trust in God, to cause us to question His goodness, and to weaken our resolve to follow Him.

However, when we take up the shield of faith, we are able to deflect these attacks. Faith in God's promises and His character acts as a buffer, absorbing the impact of the enemy's assaults and preventing them from penetrating our hearts and minds. Just as the Roman shield was large enough to cover the entire body, faith is sufficient to protect every aspect of our lives. It guards our thoughts, emotions, decisions, and actions, ensuring that we remain steadfast in our commitment to God.

Extinguishing the Flaming Arrows of the Evil One

Paul specifically mentions that the shield of faith can extinguish "all the flaming arrows of the evil one." This vivid imagery draws from the tactics used in ancient warfare, where arrows were often dipped in pitch, set on fire, and shot at the enemy. These flaming arrows were designed not only to pierce the body but also to cause widespread panic and confusion as the fire spread.

In a spiritual sense, the flaming arrows of the evil one represent the various forms of attack that Satan uses against believers. These can include doubts that cause us to question God's faithfulness, fears that paralyze us and prevent us from moving forward in our walk with God, lies that distort our understanding of who God is and who we are in Him, and temptations that lure us away from God's will.

Doubt is one of the most potent flaming arrows that the enemy uses. Doubt can cause us to question the very foundation of our faith—God's existence, His love for us, and His promises. When we face difficult circumstances or unanswered prayers, doubt can creep in, whispering lies that God is not trustworthy, that He does not care, or that He is not powerful enough to intervene. These doubts, if left unchecked, can erode our faith and lead us away from God.

However, the shield of faith can extinguish these doubts. When we hold onto the truth of God's Word and the promises He has made, we can counter the doubts with faith. For example, when we are tempted to doubt God's love for us, we can remind ourselves of Romans 8:38-39, which assures us that nothing can separate us from the love of God that is in Christ Jesus our Lord. When we are tempted to doubt God's provision, we can stand on Philippians 4:19, which promises that God will supply all our needs according to His riches in glory.

Fear is another flaming arrow that the enemy frequently uses. Fear can take many forms—fear of the future, fear of failure, fear of rejection, or fear of persecution. Fear can immobilize us, preventing us from stepping out in faith and doing what God has called us to do. It can also cause us to shrink back from opportunities to share the Gospel, to stand up for truth, or to trust God in difficult situations.

The shield of faith protects us from fear by reminding us that God is with us, that He is in control, and that His perfect love casts out fear (1 John 4:18). When we face fear, we can hold up the shield of faith and declare, "The Lord is my light and my salvation—whom shall I fear? The Lord is the stronghold of my life—of whom shall I be afraid?" (Psalm 27:1). This declaration of faith extinguishes the flaming arrow of fear and enables us to move forward with confidence.

Lies are perhaps the most insidious of the enemy's flaming arrows. Satan is described in the Bible as the father of lies (John 8:44), and his primary strategy is to distort the truth and deceive believers. These lies can take many forms—false teachings, twisted interpretations of Scripture, or subtle distortions of the truth. The enemy seeks to undermine our understanding of God's character, to make us believe that God is not who He says He is, and to convince us that we are not who God says we are.

The shield of faith is our defense against these lies. When we know the truth of God's Word and trust in His character, we can discern the enemy's lies and reject them. For example, when the enemy tries to convince us that we are unworthy of God's love, we can hold up the shield of faith and declare, "There is now no condemnation for those who are in Christ Jesus" (Romans 8:1). When the enemy tries to sow seeds of division in the body of Christ, we can stand on the truth that we are all one in Christ Jesus (Galatians 3:28).

Temptation is another form of flaming arrow that the enemy uses to lead us away from God's will. Temptation appeals to our fleshly desires and seeks to lure us into sin. The enemy often presents sin as something desirable or harmless, but the reality is that sin leads to spiritual death and separation from God. Temptation is a powerful weapon in the enemy's arsenal, but the shield of faith can protect us from it.

When we face temptation, the shield of faith reminds us of God's promises and empowers us to resist. Paul writes, "No temptation has overtaken you except what is common to mankind. And God is faithful; he will not let you be tempted beyond what you can bear. But when you are tempted, he will also provide a way out so that you can endure it" (1 Corinthians 10:13). This promise of God's faithfulness strengthens our faith and gives us the courage to stand firm against temptation.

The Importance of Faith in God's Promises

One of the key aspects of faith as a shield is its reliance on the promises of God. The Bible is filled with promises that God has made to His people—promises of protection, provision, guidance, peace, and eternal life. These promises are not just words on a page; they are the very foundation of our faith. When we trust in God's promises, we are able to stand firm in the face of spiritual attacks, knowing that God is faithful and that He will fulfill His Word.

Faith in God's promises is crucial because it gives us the assurance that, no matter what we face, God is with us and He will see us through. For example, in times of uncertainty, we can stand on the promise of Proverbs 3:5-6, which says, "Trust in the Lord with all your heart and lean not on your own understanding; in all your ways submit to him, and he will make your paths straight." This promise assures us that God is guiding our steps and that He will direct our paths according to His perfect will.

In times of fear, we can hold onto the promise of Isaiah 41:10, where God says, "So do not fear, for I am with you; do not be dismayed, for I am your God. I will strengthen you and help you; I will uphold you with my righteous right hand." This promise reminds us that God is our strength and our protector, and that we have nothing to fear when we trust in Him.

In times of need, we can rely on the promise of Philippians 4:19, which declares, "And my God will meet all your needs according to the riches of his glory in Christ Jesus." This promise assures us that God is our provider and that He will supply all our needs according to His riches in glory.

Faith in God's promises is not just about mental assent; it is about actively trusting in those promises and living in light of them. It is about holding up the shield of faith and declaring, "I believe that God is who He says He is, and I trust that He will do what He has promised to do." This kind of faith is powerful because it enables us to stand firm in the face of spiritual attacks, knowing that our God is faithful and that His promises are sure.

Faith in God's Character

In addition to trusting in God's promises, the shield of faith also involves trusting in God's character. The Bible reveals God as a loving, faithful, just, and all-powerful God who is worthy of our trust. When we place our faith in God's character, we are able to withstand the attacks of the enemy because we know that God is for us and that He will never leave us nor forsake us.

Trusting in God's character is essential because the enemy often tries to distort our understanding of who God is. He may try to convince us that God is distant, uncaring, or untrustworthy. He may try to make us believe that God is harsh, punitive, or quick to anger. But when we hold up the shield of faith, we are able to reject these lies and stand firm in the truth of who God is.

For example, when the enemy tries to make us doubt God's goodness, we can hold up the shield of faith and declare, "The Lord is good, a refuge in times of trouble. He cares for those who trust in him" (Nahum 1:7). When the enemy tries to make us believe that God is unfaithful, we can stand on the truth that "God is faithful, who has called you into fellowship with his Son, Jesus Christ our Lord" (1 Corinthians 1:9).

Faith in God's character also involves trusting in His sovereignty. The Bible teaches that God is in control of all things and that nothing happens outside of His will. This means that, even when we face difficult or painful circumstances, we can trust that God is working all things together for our good (Romans 8:28). This trust in God's sovereignty gives us the confidence to stand firm, even when we do not understand why certain things are happening or how they will work out.

The story of Job is a powerful example of faith in God's character. Despite losing everything—his wealth, his family, and his health—Job refused to curse God or abandon his faith. Instead, he declared, "Though he slay me, yet will I hope in him" (Job 13:15). Job's faith in God's character allowed him to endure the most intense trials and to come out of them with his faith intact.

This kind of faith is what enables us to withstand the attacks of the enemy. When we trust in God's character—His goodness, His faithfulness, His love, and His sovereignty—we are able to stand firm, knowing that God is for us and that He will see us through whatever challenges we face.

The Communal Aspect of Faith as a Shield

While the shield of faith is a deeply personal piece of spiritual armor, there is also a communal aspect to it. Just as Roman soldiers would lock their shields together to form an impenetrable wall, Christians are called to support one another in faith, standing together against the attacks of the enemy.

The Bible teaches that we are not meant to fight spiritual battles alone. We are part of the body of Christ, and we are called to encourage, support, and build one another up in faith. Paul writes, "Therefore encourage one another and build each other up, just as in fact you are doing" (1 Thessalonians 5:11). When we stand together in faith, we create a strong defense against the enemy's attacks.

This communal aspect of faith is seen in the way that believers are called to pray for one another. James writes, "Therefore confess your sins to each other and pray for each other so that you may be healed. The prayer of a righteous person is powerful and effective" (James 5:16). When we pray for one another, we are lifting up the shield of faith on behalf of our brothers and sisters in Christ, helping to protect them from the enemy's attacks.

The early church provides a powerful example of the communal aspect of faith as a shield. In the book of Acts, we see the believers gathered together in prayer, supporting one another in faith, and standing firm in the face of persecution. Acts 4:31 describes how, after they prayed, "the place where they were meeting was shaken. And they were all filled with the Holy Spirit and spoke the word of God boldly." Their faith was not only personal but also collective, and it gave them the strength to stand firm in the face of intense opposition.

In the same way, we are called to stand together in faith, supporting one another and helping each other to hold up the shield of faith. When one member of the body is struggling, the others can come alongside them, offering encouragement, prayer, and support. This communal aspect of faith is essential for our spiritual growth and for our ability to withstand the attacks of the enemy.

Faith and the Word of God

The shield of faith is closely connected to the Word of God. The Bible teaches that "faith comes from hearing, and hearing through the word of Christ" (Romans 10:17). This means that our faith is strengthened and sustained by our engagement with Scripture. The more we immerse ourselves in God's Word, the stronger our faith becomes, and the better equipped we are to withstand spiritual attacks.

The Word of God is the foundation of our faith because it reveals who God is, what He has done, and what He promises to do. It provides the truth that we need to stand against the lies of the enemy, and it gives us the promises that we can hold onto in times of trial. When we meditate on God's Word and allow it to shape our thoughts and attitudes, our faith is fortified, and we are able to hold up the shield of faith with confidence.

Jesus Himself demonstrated the power of the Word of God in spiritual warfare during His temptation in the wilderness. When Satan tempted Him, Jesus responded by quoting Scripture, saying, "It is written..." (Matthew 4:4, 7, 10). Jesus' faith in the truth of God's Word enabled Him to resist the enemy's attacks and to stand firm in His mission.

In the same way, we are called to use the Word of God as a weapon in spiritual warfare. When the enemy attacks us with doubts, fears, or lies, we can hold up the shield of faith by declaring, "It is written..." and standing on the truth of God's Word. This is why it is so important for us to know Scripture, to meditate on it, and to hide it in our hearts. The Word of God is our source of strength, and it is what enables us to hold up the shield of faith with confidence.

Faith and Prayer

Prayer is another essential component of the shield of faith. Through prayer, we communicate with God, express our trust in Him, and invite Him to intervene in our lives. Prayer is an act of faith because it acknowledges our dependence on God and our belief that He hears and answers our prayers.

The Bible teaches that "the prayer of faith will save the one who is sick, and the Lord will raise him up" (James 5:15). This means that our prayers, when offered in faith, have the power to bring about real change. Prayer is a way of holding up the shield of faith, inviting God to protect us from the enemy's attacks and to provide for our needs.

In Ephesians 6, after describing the armor of God, Paul exhorts believers to "pray in the Spirit on all occasions with all kinds of prayers and requests. With this in mind, be alert and always keep on praying for all the Lord's people" (Ephesians 6:18). Prayer is the means by which we activate the armor of God, including the shield of faith. It is through prayer that we express our trust in God's protection, our reliance on His promises, and our confidence in His character.

When we pray in faith, we are holding up the shield of faith and inviting God to be our defense. We are declaring our trust in His power, His wisdom, and His love, and we are asking Him to intervene in our circumstances. Prayer is not just a ritual or a routine; it is a powerful act of faith that connects us with the living God and invites Him to move on our behalf.

Growing in Faith

The shield of faith is not static; it is something that can grow and strengthen over time. Just as a soldier's shield may become stronger and more effective with use, our faith can grow as we walk with God and experience His faithfulness in our lives.

The Bible teaches that faith is a gift from God, but it is also something that we are called to cultivate and develop. In 2 Peter 1:5-8, Peter exhorts believers to "make every effort to add to your faith goodness; and to goodness, knowledge; and to knowledge, self-control; and to self-control, perseverance; and to perseverance, godliness; and to godliness, mutual affection; and to mutual affection, love." This passage reminds us that faith is the foundation of our spiritual growth, but it is also something that we are called to actively develop.

One way to grow in faith is by spending time in God's Word, as we have already discussed. The more we immerse ourselves in Scripture, the more our faith is strengthened, and the better equipped we are to hold up the shield of faith. Another way to grow in faith is through prayer, as we invite God to work in our lives and trust Him to answer our prayers.

We can also grow in faith by stepping out in obedience to God's leading. When we take steps of faith, even when we do not have all the answers or when the outcome is uncertain, we give God the opportunity to demonstrate His faithfulness. As we see God come through for us in these situations, our faith is strengthened, and we become more confident in His ability to protect and provide for us.

Finally, we can grow in faith by surrounding ourselves with other believers who can encourage us, challenge us, and support us in our walk with God. The communal aspect of faith is essential for our spiritual growth, as it provides us with the support and accountability we need to continue growing in our faith.

Conclusion: Taking Up the Shield of Faith

As we conclude this reflection on the shield of faith, it is important to remember that faith is not just a concept or a feeling; it is an active, living trust in God. The shield of faith is a powerful piece of spiritual armor that protects us from the enemy's attacks, extinguishes the flaming arrows of doubt, fear, and lies, and enables us to stand firm in our walk with God.

Taking up the shield of faith means trusting in God's promises, relying on His character, and standing on the truth of His Word. It means engaging in prayer, surrounding ourselves with other believers, and stepping out in obedience to God's leading. As we do these things, our faith is strengthened, and we become more effective in our spiritual warfare.

The shield of faith is not something that we take up once and then forget about; it is something that we must continually hold up, day by day, moment by moment. It is our defense against the enemy's attacks and our source of strength in the midst of spiritual battles.

Let us, therefore, take up the shield of faith with confidence, trusting in the God who is faithful, who loves us, and who has promised to be with us always. As we do, we will find that the shield of faith is more than sufficient to protect us, to strengthen us, and to lead us to victory in Christ.

Chapter 5: The Helmet of Salvation

Theme: The assurance of salvation protecting the mind.

Reflection: Reflect on the importance of the helmet of salvation in guarding our thoughts and minds. Discuss how the assurance of salvation in Christ protects us from the enemy's attempts to plant seeds of doubt and fear.

In the Apostle Paul's vivid depiction of the armor of God, each piece carries profound significance, not only as a metaphor for the Christian's spiritual defense but also as a vital component of our daily walk with Christ. Among these, the helmet of salvation stands out as a crucial piece of armor, designed to protect the mind from the relentless assaults of the enemy. In this chapter, we will explore the symbolism and significance of the helmet of salvation, examining how the assurance of our salvation in Christ serves as a powerful defense against doubt, fear, and the lies of the enemy.

The Roman Helmet: A Historical Context

To fully understand the metaphor of the helmet of salvation, it is helpful to consider the historical context of the Roman helmet, or "galea." The galea was an essential part of a Roman soldier's armor, crafted from metal or leather and often lined with felt or sponge for comfort. The helmet was designed to protect the soldier's head from blows and projectiles, safeguarding the most vital and vulnerable part of the body. In battle, a head injury could be fatal, so the helmet was indispensable for survival.

The helmet typically covered the entire head, including the back and sides, and was often fitted with a chin strap to ensure it stayed securely in place during combat. Some helmets were adorned with a crest or plume, symbolizing rank or unit, but regardless of the design, the primary purpose of the helmet was protection. Without a helmet, a soldier would be vulnerable to fatal injuries, rendering the rest of his armor ineffective.

In the same way, the helmet of salvation is essential for the Christian in spiritual warfare. It protects the mind, the seat of our thoughts, beliefs, and decisions, from the enemy's attacks. Just as the Roman helmet was designed to withstand the force of a sword or spear, the helmet of salvation is designed to withstand the psychological and spiritual attacks that Satan directs at the mind. Without this protection, we are vulnerable to doubt, fear, and confusion, which can lead us away from the truth of the Gospel and the security of our salvation in Christ.

The Mind: The Battlefield of Spiritual Warfare

The mind is the primary battlefield in spiritual warfare. It is in our thoughts that the enemy often wages his most intense battles, seeking to influence our beliefs, distort our perceptions, and lead us into sin. The Bible teaches that as a man thinks in his heart, so is he (Proverbs 23:7). This means that our thoughts have a profound impact on our actions, our attitudes, and our spiritual well-being.

The enemy knows that if he can control our minds, he can control our lives. This is why the helmet of salvation is so critical—it protects our minds from the enemy's attempts to plant seeds of doubt, fear, and deception. When we wear the helmet of salvation, we are guarding our minds with the truth of God's Word and the assurance of our salvation in Christ.

One of the primary ways that the enemy attacks the mind is through lies. Jesus described Satan as the father of lies (John 8:44), and his strategy has always been to deceive and distort the truth. In the Garden of Eden, Satan's first attack on humanity was through deception. He questioned God's Word and planted seeds of doubt in Eve's mind, leading her to disobey God's command. This pattern of deception continues today, as the enemy seeks to undermine our faith by distorting the truth and causing us to question God's promises.

The helmet of salvation protects us from these lies by reminding us of the truth of our salvation. When we are secure in our salvation, we can resist the enemy's attempts to deceive us. We can stand firm in the knowledge that we are saved by grace through faith in Christ, and that nothing can separate us from the love of God (Romans 8:38-39). This assurance of salvation is a powerful defense against the enemy's lies, enabling us to reject falsehood and cling to the truth.

The Assurance of Salvation: A Firm Foundation

The helmet of salvation represents the assurance of our salvation in Christ. This assurance is not based on our own efforts or righteousness, but on the finished work of Jesus on the cross. The Bible teaches that we are saved by grace through faith, and that this salvation is a gift from God, not a result of our works (Ephesians 2:8-9). Because our salvation is grounded in the unchanging character of God and the completed work of Christ, we can have confidence and security in our relationship with God.

This assurance is a firm foundation that protects us from the enemy's attempts to cause us to doubt our salvation. Doubt is one of the most effective weapons that Satan uses against believers. He seeks to make us question whether we are truly saved, whether God truly loves us, and whether we are truly forgiven. These doubts can lead to fear, anxiety, and spiritual paralysis, hindering our ability to live out our faith and fulfill God's calling on our lives.

However, when we wear the helmet of salvation, we are reminded of the truth that our salvation is secure in Christ. Jesus said, "My sheep listen to my voice; I know them, and they follow me. I give them eternal life, and they shall never perish; no one will snatch them out of my hand" (John 10:27-28). This promise gives us the confidence that, once we have placed our faith in Christ, our salvation is secure and cannot be taken away.

The assurance of salvation also protects us from the fear of judgment. The Bible teaches that there is no condemnation for those who are in Christ Jesus (Romans 8:1). This means that, because of Christ's sacrifice on the cross, we are no longer under the penalty of sin, and we do not need to fear God's judgment. This assurance frees us from the fear of death and the fear of the future, enabling us to live with confidence and peace, knowing that our eternity is secure in Christ.

Guarding the Mind Against Doubt and Fear

The helmet of salvation not only provides assurance but also guards our minds against doubt and fear. Doubt and fear are two of the most common and destructive attacks that the enemy uses against believers. They can cause us to waver in our faith, to question God's goodness, and to become discouraged and disheartened in our walk with Christ.

Doubt often begins with a subtle question: "Did God really say…?" This was the tactic that Satan used in the Garden of Eden, and it is the same tactic he uses today. He plants seeds of doubt in our minds, causing us to question God's Word, His promises, and His character. Doubt can lead us down a dangerous path, where we begin to rely on our own understanding rather than trusting in God's wisdom and guidance.

The helmet of salvation protects us from doubt by reminding us of the truth of God's Word and the security of our salvation. When we are tempted to doubt, we can hold onto the promises of Scripture, which assure us of God's faithfulness and His love for us. For example, when we doubt God's love, we can turn to Romans 5:8, which says, "But God demonstrates his own love for us in this: While we were still sinners, Christ died for us." This verse reminds us that God's love is unconditional and that He has already proven His love for us through the sacrifice of His Son.

Fear is another powerful weapon that the enemy uses to attack the mind. Fear can paralyze us, preventing us from stepping out in faith and following God's leading. It can cause us to shrink back from challenges, to avoid risks, and to miss out on the opportunities that God has placed before us. Fear can also lead to anxiety, worry, and stress, which can take a toll on our mental, emotional, and spiritual well-being.

The helmet of salvation protects us from fear by reminding us that God is with us, that He is in control, and that He has a plan and purpose for our lives. The Bible is filled with promises that speak to God's protection and provision, and these promises give us the courage to face our fears with confidence. For example, in Isaiah 41:10, God says, "So do not fear, for I am with you; do not be dismayed, for I am your God. I will strengthen you and help you; I will uphold you with my righteous right hand." This verse reminds us that we do not need to fear because God is our protector and our provider.

The Power of a Renewed Mind

The helmet of salvation not only protects the mind but also plays a vital role in the process of renewing the mind. The Bible teaches that, as believers, we are called to be transformed by the renewing of our minds (Romans 12:2). This renewal is a continual process of aligning our thoughts, beliefs, and attitudes with the truth of God's Word, and it is essential for our spiritual growth and maturity.

A renewed mind is a mind that is rooted in the truth of the Gospel and the assurance of salvation. It is a mind that is focused on the things of God, rather than the things of this world. It is a mind that is filled with the peace of Christ, rather than the anxieties and fears that the enemy seeks to impose.

The process of renewing the mind involves several key steps:

1. Meditating on God's Word: The first step in renewing the mind is to immerse ourselves in Scripture. The Bible is the ultimate source of truth, and it is through the study and meditation on God's Word that we come to know His character, His promises, and His will for our lives. Psalm 1:2-3 says, "But whose delight is in the law of the Lord, and who meditates on his law day and night. That person is like a tree planted by streams of water, which yields its fruit in season and whose leaf does not wither—whatever they do prospers." By meditating on God's Word, we are feeding our minds with the truth and allowing it to take root in our hearts.

2. Taking Every Thought Captive: The second step in renewing the mind is to take every thought captive and make it obedient to Christ (2 Corinthians 10:5). This means that we are to evaluate our thoughts in light of Scripture and reject any thought that is contrary to God's Word. When we are confronted with doubts, fears, or negative thoughts, we can counter them with the truth of Scripture and choose to believe what God says rather than what our circumstances or feelings may suggest.

3. Focusing on What is True: The third step in renewing the mind is to focus on what is true, noble, right, pure, lovely, admirable, excellent, and praiseworthy (Philippians 4:8). This means that we are to fill our minds with positive and edifying thoughts that align with God's character and His will. By focusing on these things, we are training our minds to think in a way that honors God and reflects His truth.

4. Practicing Gratitude: The fourth step in renewing the mind is to cultivate an attitude of gratitude. Gratitude shifts our focus from what we lack to what we have been given, and it reminds us of God's goodness and faithfulness. When we practice gratitude, we are acknowledging God's blessings in our lives

and recognizing His hand at work. This attitude of gratitude helps to guard our minds against the enemy's attempts to sow seeds of discontent, envy, or despair.

5. Praying for a Renewed Mind: The final step in renewing the mind is to pray for God's help in this process. We can ask God to renew our minds, to help us to think in a way that is pleasing to Him, and to protect our minds from the enemy's attacks. Psalm 139:23-24 says, "Search me, God, and know my heart; test me and know my anxious thoughts. See if there is any offensive way in me, and lead me in the way everlasting." This prayer invites God to examine our thoughts and to lead us in His truth.

A renewed mind is essential for our spiritual health and well-being. It enables us to discern God's will, to resist the enemy's attacks, and to live in a way that is pleasing to God. The helmet of salvation plays a vital role in this renewal process by protecting our minds from the enemy's attempts to distort our thinking and by reminding us of the truth of our salvation.

The Role of Hope in the Helmet of Salvation

The helmet of salvation is not only about the assurance of our current salvation but also about the hope of our future salvation. In 1 Thessalonians 5:8, Paul writes, "But since we belong to the day, let us be sober, putting on faith and love as a breastplate, and the hope of salvation as a helmet." This verse highlights the importance of hope in the Christian life and how it serves as a vital component of the helmet of salvation.

Hope is a confident expectation of what God has promised, and it is rooted in His faithfulness. The hope of salvation is the assurance that, because of what Christ has done, we have the promise of eternal life with God. This hope is not wishful thinking; it is a firm and certain expectation based on the truth of God's Word.

The hope of salvation protects our minds from the despair and discouragement that the enemy seeks to impose. In times of trial, suffering, or uncertainty, the hope of salvation reminds us that our current circumstances are temporary and that our ultimate destiny is secure in Christ. This hope gives us the strength to persevere, to endure hardships, and to remain faithful to God, even when the road is difficult.

The hope of salvation also motivates us to live holy and righteous lives. In 1 John 3:2-3, we read, "Dear friends, now we are children of God, and what we will be has not yet been made known. But we know that when Christ appears, we shall be like him, for we shall see him as he is. All who have this hope in him purify themselves, just as he is pure." The hope of salvation inspires us to live in a way that reflects our identity as children of God and our anticipation of Christ's return.

Hope is a powerful force that sustains us through the challenges of life. When we put on the helmet of salvation, we are not only guarding our minds with the assurance of our current salvation but also with the hope of our future salvation. This hope enables us to keep our eyes fixed on Jesus, the author and perfecter of our faith (Hebrews 12:2), and to run the race with endurance.

Overcoming the Accusations of the Enemy

One of the most common ways that the enemy attacks the mind is through accusations. The Bible describes Satan as the accuser of the brethren (Revelation 12:10), and his goal is to make us feel condemned, guilty, and unworthy of God's love and grace. These accusations can be relentless, causing us to doubt our salvation, question our worth, and feel defeated in our walk with Christ.

The helmet of salvation is a powerful defense against these accusations. When we are secure in our salvation, we can stand firm against the enemy's attempts to condemn us. We can remind ourselves that our salvation is not based on our own righteousness but on the righteousness of Christ. Isaiah 61:10 says, "I delight greatly in the Lord; my soul rejoices in my God. For he has clothed me with garments of salvation and arrayed me in a robe of his righteousness." This verse reminds us that we are clothed in the righteousness of Christ and that our salvation is secure because of what He has done, not because of what we have done.

When the enemy accuses us of our past sins, we can respond with the truth of 1 John 1:9, which says, "If we confess our sins, he is faithful and just and will forgive us our sins and purify us from all unrighteousness." This verse assures us that when we confess our sins, God forgives us and cleanses us from all unrighteousness. We do not need to carry the burden of guilt and shame because Christ has already paid the penalty for our sins, and we are forgiven.

The helmet of salvation also protects us from the enemy's attempts to make us feel unworthy of God's love. Ephesians 2:4-5 says, "But because of his great love for us, God, who is rich in mercy, made us alive with Christ even when we were dead in transgressions—it is by grace you have been saved." This verse reminds us that God's love for us is not based on our worthiness but on His grace. We are loved and accepted by God because of His great mercy, not because of anything we have done.

The accusations of the enemy are designed to weaken our faith and to cause us to doubt our salvation. But when we wear the helmet of salvation, we can stand firm in the truth of God's Word and reject these accusations. We can remind ourselves that we are saved by grace, that we are clothed in the righteousness of Christ, and that we are loved and accepted by God. This truth gives us the confidence to resist the enemy's attacks and to live in the freedom and joy of our salvation.

The Helmet of Salvation in Daily Life

The helmet of salvation is not just a metaphorical piece of armor; it is a practical tool that we can use in our daily lives to protect our minds and to strengthen our faith. Here are some ways that we can apply the helmet of salvation in our everyday lives:

1. Daily Reminders of Salvation: One way to apply the helmet of salvation is to remind ourselves daily of the truth of our salvation. This can be done through prayer, meditation on Scripture, or even simple affirmations of faith. For example, we can begin each day by thanking God for His gift of salvation and by declaring our trust in His promises. This daily reminder helps to keep our minds focused on the truth and to guard against the enemy's attacks.

2. Rejecting Negative Thoughts: Another way to apply the helmet of salvation is to actively reject negative thoughts that do not align with the truth of God's Word. When we are confronted with thoughts of doubt, fear, or condemnation, we can take them captive and replace them with the truth of Scripture. For example, if we are tempted to doubt God's love, we can remind

ourselves of Romans 8:38-39, which assures us that nothing can separate us from the love of God in Christ Jesus.

3. Focusing on Eternal Perspective: The helmet of salvation also helps us to maintain an eternal perspective in our daily lives. When we are faced with challenges or difficulties, we can remind ourselves that our ultimate hope is in Christ and that our current circumstances are temporary. This eternal perspective helps us to endure trials with patience and to remain steadfast in our faith.

4. Cultivating a Grateful Heart: Gratitude is a powerful way to apply the helmet of salvation. When we cultivate a heart of gratitude, we are acknowledging God's blessings in our lives and recognizing His hand at work. This attitude of gratitude helps to guard our minds against the enemy's attempts to sow seeds of discontent, envy, or despair.

5. Engaging in Worship: Worship is another way to apply the helmet of salvation. When we engage in worship, we are lifting our minds and hearts to God, focusing on His greatness and His goodness. Worship helps to strengthen our faith and to renew our minds, filling us with the peace and joy of God's presence.

Conclusion: Wearing the Helmet of Salvation

As we conclude this reflection on the helmet of salvation, it is important to remember that this piece of armor is essential for our spiritual protection and well-being. The helmet of salvation guards our minds against the enemy's attacks, providing us with the assurance of our salvation, the hope of our future, and the power to renew our minds.

Wearing the helmet of salvation means living each day in the confidence and security of our salvation in Christ. It means rejecting the lies and accusations of the enemy and standing firm in the truth of God's Word. It means focusing our minds on the things of God, cultivating an attitude of gratitude, and engaging in worship.

The helmet of salvation is not something we put on once and then forget about; it is something we must wear continually, day by day, moment by moment. It is our defense against the enemy's attempts to plant seeds of doubt, fear, and deception in our minds. It is our protection as we navigate the challenges of life and seek to live in a way that honors God.

Let us, therefore, take up the helmet of salvation with confidence, trusting in the God who has saved us, who loves us, and who has promised to be with us always. As we do, we will find that the helmet of salvation is more than sufficient to protect us, to strengthen us, and to lead us to victory in Christ.

Chapter 6: The Sword of the Spirit

Theme: The Word of God as an offensive weapon.

Reflection: Explore the role of the Word of God as the only offensive weapon in spiritual warfare. Reflect on how Scripture can be used to counter the lies of the enemy, offering examples of how Jesus used Scripture in His own battles against temptation.

In the Apostle Paul's description of the armor of God found in Ephesians 6, the sword of the Spirit stands out as the only offensive weapon in the believer's arsenal. While the other pieces of armor—such as the helmet, breastplate, and shield—are designed primarily for defense, the sword of the Spirit is meant for active engagement in spiritual warfare. This sword, which is the Word of God, is a powerful weapon in the hands of a believer, enabling us to counter the lies and attacks of the enemy with truth and authority.

In this chapter, we will explore the significance of the sword of the Spirit as the Word of God, examining how it functions as an offensive weapon in spiritual warfare. We will reflect on the power of Scripture to defeat the enemy, offering examples of how Jesus Himself used Scripture to overcome temptation. Finally, we will discuss practical ways to wield the sword of the Spirit effectively in our own lives.

The Nature of the Sword of the Spirit

To understand the significance of the sword of the Spirit, it is helpful to consider the nature of a sword in both historical and spiritual contexts. In the ancient world, the sword was a versatile and deadly weapon, used by soldiers for both offense and defense. A skilled swordsman could parry the attacks of an enemy, as well as deliver precise and powerful strikes. The Roman soldiers, whom Paul likely had in mind when he wrote about the armor of God, used a short sword called a "gladius." This sword was designed for close combat, allowing the soldier to engage the enemy with precision and speed.

In the spiritual realm, the sword of the Spirit represents the Word of God, which is described in Hebrews 4:12 as "living and active, sharper than any double-edged sword, it penetrates even to dividing soul and spirit, joints and marrow; it judges the thoughts and attitudes of the heart." The Word of God is not a passive or inert text; it is dynamic, powerful, and capable of penetrating the deepest parts of our being. It reveals truth, exposes lies, convicts of sin, and brings about transformation.

The sword of the Spirit is unique among the pieces of the armor of God because it is both defensive and offensive. It can be used to fend off the enemy's attacks, as well as to launch counterattacks. While the shield of faith can extinguish the flaming arrows of the evil one, the sword of the Spirit can strike back, cutting through the deception and lies of the enemy with the truth of God's Word.

The Word of God as the Foundation of Truth

Central to the effectiveness of the sword of the Spirit is the nature of the Word of God as the ultimate source of truth. In a world where truth is often relative and subjective, the Bible stands as the unchanging and authoritative revelation of God's will and character. Jesus prayed to the Father, "Sanctify them by the truth; your word is truth" (John 17:17). The Word of God is the standard by which all other truths are measured, and it is the foundation upon which we build our faith and conduct our spiritual warfare.

The enemy, whom Jesus called the "father of lies" (John 8:44), thrives on deception and falsehood. His primary tactic is to distort the truth, to twist God's Word, and to sow seeds of doubt in the hearts of believers. This was evident in the Garden of Eden, where Satan's first recorded words to humanity were a question designed to undermine God's truth: "Did God really say...?" (Genesis 3:1). This tactic has not changed; the enemy continues to challenge and distort God's Word in an attempt to lead believers astray.

However, when we wield the sword of the Spirit—the Word of God—we have a powerful weapon against the enemy's lies. The truth of Scripture exposes the deception of the enemy and provides clarity in the midst of confusion. It serves as a light that guides our path (Psalm 119:105), enabling us to discern right from wrong and to stand firm in the midst of spiritual battles.

Jesus' Use of Scripture in Spiritual Warfare

One of the most powerful examples of the sword of the Spirit in action is found in the life of Jesus. In the wilderness, after fasting for forty days and forty nights, Jesus faced a series of temptations from Satan. Each time, Jesus responded to the enemy's attacks not with physical force or human reasoning, but with Scripture. This encounter, recorded in Matthew 4:1-11 and Luke 4:1-13, provides a profound example of how the Word of God can be used to counter the lies and temptations of the enemy.

1. The Temptation to Turn Stones into Bread:

The first temptation Satan presented to Jesus was to turn stones into bread, appealing to His physical hunger after forty days of fasting. Satan said, "If you are the Son of God, tell these stones to become bread" (Matthew 4:3). This temptation was not merely about satisfying hunger; it was a challenge to Jesus' identity and trust in God's provision.

Jesus responded by quoting Deuteronomy 8:3: "It is written: 'Man shall not live on bread alone, but on every word that comes from the mouth of God'" (Matthew 4:4). By wielding the sword of the Spirit, Jesus affirmed that true sustenance comes from God's Word, not merely from physical food. He rejected the temptation to use His divine power for self-gratification and instead reaffirmed His trust in God's provision.

2. The Temptation to Test God:

The second temptation involved Satan taking Jesus to the pinnacle of the temple and urging Him to throw Himself down, quoting Psalm 91:11-12 to suggest that God would protect Him: "If you are the Son of God, throw yourself down. For it is written: 'He will command his angels concerning you, and they will lift you up in their hands, so that you will not strike your foot against a stone'" (Matthew 4:6).

Satan's misuse of Scripture was a twisted attempt to manipulate Jesus into testing God's faithfulness. However, Jesus countered with Deuteronomy 6:16: "It is also written: 'Do not put the Lord your God to the test'" (Matthew 4:7). By using the sword of the Spirit, Jesus exposed the enemy's distortion of Scripture and reaffirmed the principle that God's promises should not be presumptuously tested.

3. The Temptation to Worship Satan:

The final temptation was the most blatant: Satan offered Jesus all the kingdoms of the world if He would bow down and worship him. This was an attempt to entice Jesus with power and glory apart from the cross.

Jesus responded with uncompromising truth, quoting Deuteronomy 6:13: "Away from me, Satan! For it is written: 'Worship the Lord your God, and serve him only'" (Matthew 4:10). With this declaration, Jesus rejected the allure of worldly power and affirmed His commitment to worship and serve God alone.

In each of these temptations, Jesus used the sword of the Spirit to counter the enemy's lies. He did not engage in debate or rely on His own reasoning; instead, He wielded the Word of God with precision and authority. This example demonstrates the power of Scripture to defeat the enemy and the importance of knowing and applying God's Word in our own spiritual battles.

The Power of the Word in Spiritual Warfare

The Word of God is not just a collection of ancient texts; it is a living and active weapon in the hands of a believer. When we speak or declare God's Word in faith, it has the power to change circumstances, to bring about spiritual breakthroughs, and to defeat the enemy. This is because the Word of God carries the authority of the One who spoke it—God Himself.

In Isaiah 55:11, God declares, "So is my word that goes out from my mouth: It will not return to me empty, but will accomplish what I desire and achieve the purpose for which I sent it." This verse highlights the effectiveness of God's Word; it always accomplishes His purposes. When we wield the sword of the Spirit, we are aligning ourselves with God's will and His purposes, and we can trust that His Word will achieve what He has intended.

The power of the Word in spiritual warfare is evident throughout Scripture. In the Old Testament, we see examples of God's Word bringing victory in battle, as in the case of Joshua and the battle of Jericho (Joshua 6). God's instructions to Joshua were clear, and as the Israelites obeyed and acted in faith, the walls of Jericho fell by the power of God's Word.

In the New Testament, the early church experienced the power of God's Word as they spread the Gospel and faced opposition. In Acts 4:31, after the believers prayed for boldness, "the place where they were meeting was shaken. And they were all filled with the Holy Spirit and spoke the word of God boldly." The bold proclamation of God's Word resulted in the spread of the Gospel and the defeat of the enemy's attempts to silence the church.

The power of the Word in spiritual warfare is not limited to biblical times; it is available to us today. When we declare God's Word over our lives, our circumstances, and our battles, we are wielding the sword of the Spirit and aligning ourselves with God's authority. This is not a matter of "name it and claim it" theology, but rather a recognition that God's Word is powerful and effective, and that it is our responsibility to speak and stand on that Word in faith.

Using the Sword of the Spirit in Our Lives

To effectively wield the sword of the Spirit in our lives, we must first know the Word of God. This requires a commitment to studying, meditating on, and memorizing Scripture. The psalmist declared, "I have hidden your word in my heart that I might not sin against you" (Psalm 119:11). Hiding God's Word in our hearts means internalizing it so that it becomes a part of us—our thoughts, our beliefs, and our responses.

1. Studying the Word:

To wield the sword of the Spirit effectively, we must be diligent students of the Word. This involves regular and intentional study of Scripture, seeking to understand its meaning, context, and application. The Bible is a vast and rich text, and studying it allows us to gain a deeper understanding of God's character, His promises, and His commands. As Paul instructed Timothy, "Do your best to present yourself to God as one approved, a worker who does not need to be ashamed and who correctly handles the word of truth" (2 Timothy 2:15).

Studying the Word also involves seeking the guidance of the Holy Spirit, who is the ultimate author and interpreter of Scripture. Jesus promised that the Holy Spirit would "teach you all things and will remind you of everything I have said to you" (John 14:26). As we study the Word, we should pray for the Holy Spirit to open our minds and hearts to understand and apply its truths.

2. Meditating on the Word:

Meditation on Scripture goes beyond mere reading or study; it involves pondering and reflecting on God's Word, allowing it to saturate our minds and hearts. In Joshua 1:8, God instructed Joshua, "Keep this Book of the Law always on your lips; meditate on it day and night, so that you may be careful to do everything written in it. Then you will be prosperous and successful." Meditation on God's Word helps us to internalize its truths and to apply them to our daily lives.

Meditation also involves speaking God's Word out loud, declaring its truths over our circumstances and aligning our thoughts with God's thoughts. As we meditate on Scripture, we are training our minds to think in accordance with God's Word, which is essential for effective spiritual warfare.

3. Memorizing the Word:

Memorizing Scripture is a powerful way to equip ourselves with the sword of the Spirit. When we commit God's Word to memory, we are arming ourselves with truth that can be readily accessed in times of need. Jesus' responses to Satan's temptations were all drawn from Scripture that He had memorized. In the same way, when we memorize Scripture, we are preparing ourselves to counter the enemy's attacks with the truth.

Memorization also allows us to meditate on Scripture throughout the day, even when we do not have a Bible in front of us. It enables us to recall God's promises, to pray His Word, and to encourage ourselves and others with truth. As the psalmist declared, "I will not forget your word" (Psalm 119:16).

4. Praying the Word:

One of the most effective ways to wield the sword of the Spirit is through prayer. Praying God's Word involves incorporating Scripture into our prayers, declaring His promises, and aligning our requests with His will. The Bible is filled with prayers that we can use as models, as well as promises that we can claim in prayer.

When we pray God's Word, we are speaking His truth into our situations and inviting His power to work on our behalf. For example, if we are facing fear, we can pray Psalm 27:1, "The Lord is my light and my salvation—whom shall I fear? The Lord is the stronghold of my life—of whom shall I be afraid?" Praying Scripture strengthens our faith and brings our hearts into alignment with God's will.

5. Declaring the Word:

Another way to wield the sword of the Spirit is through declaration. Declaring God's Word involves speaking His truth out loud, whether in times of worship, spiritual warfare, or daily life. In the face of opposition, declaring God's Word is a way of standing firm in faith and resisting the enemy's attacks.

For example, when we face temptation, we can declare 1 Corinthians 10:13, which promises that God will provide a way out of temptation. When we are tempted to worry, we can declare Philippians 4:6-7, which reminds us to present our requests to God with thanksgiving and to receive His peace. Declaring God's Word is an act of faith that releases the power of Scripture into our lives and circumstances.

The Importance of Discernment in Wielding the Sword of the Spirit

While the sword of the Spirit is a powerful weapon, it must be wielded with discernment and wisdom. Scripture can be misused, twisted, or taken out of context, as demonstrated by Satan's attempt to manipulate Psalm 91 during Jesus' temptation. To wield the sword of the Spirit effectively, we must be guided by the Holy Spirit and have a deep understanding of the Word's true meaning and application.

1. Context Matters:

One of the key principles of biblical interpretation is understanding the context in which a passage was written. This includes the historical, cultural, and literary context, as well as the surrounding verses. Misinterpreting or taking Scripture out of context can lead to error and can be used by the enemy to deceive. For example, Philippians 4:13, "I can do all this through him who gives me strength," is often quoted out of context to imply that believers can achieve any personal goal, when the context is actually about contentment in all circumstances.

To wield the sword of the Spirit with discernment, we must study Scripture in its context and seek to understand its original meaning and intent. This allows us to apply God's Word accurately and effectively in our lives.

2. The Role of the Holy Spirit:

The Holy Spirit plays a vital role in helping us wield the sword of the Spirit. Jesus promised that the Holy Spirit would guide us into all truth (John 16:13), and this includes giving us understanding and discernment as we study and apply God's Word. The Holy Spirit illuminates Scripture, helping us to see its relevance to our lives and to recognize when and how to use it in spiritual warfare.

The Holy Spirit also provides the wisdom to know when to speak and when to remain silent, when to declare a promise and when to wait on God. As we seek the guidance of the Holy Spirit, we can wield the sword of the Spirit with precision and power, using it in alignment with God's will.

3. Avoiding Legalism and Misuse:

The sword of the Spirit must be wielded with love, grace, and humility. It is possible to misuse Scripture in a legalistic or judgmental way, which can cause harm rather than healing. For example, using Scripture to condemn or manipulate others is a misuse of the sword of the Spirit. Jesus, who is the Word made flesh, wielded the sword of the Spirit with compassion and truth, not to oppress but to set people free.

We must be careful to avoid using Scripture as a weapon against others in a way that contradicts the heart of the Gospel. Instead, we should wield the sword of the Spirit to bring life, to edify, to correct with love, and to lead others to the truth of God's Word.

The Sword of the Spirit in Community

The sword of the Spirit is not just for individual use; it is also meant to be wielded in community. The early church provides a powerful example of how the Word of God can be used collectively to build up the body of Christ and to advance the kingdom of God.

1. Corporate Worship:

In corporate worship, the Word of God is proclaimed, sung, and declared. As believers gather to worship, the sword of the Spirit is wielded collectively, strengthening the faith of the community and resisting the attacks of the enemy. The public reading of Scripture, preaching, and singing of biblical truths all contribute to the collective wielding of the sword of the Spirit.

The early church devoted themselves to the apostles' teaching (Acts 2:42), and this teaching was grounded in the Word of God. As the church gathered, they were equipped with the sword of the Spirit to stand firm in their faith and to witness boldly to the world.

2. Discipleship and Teaching:

The sword of the Spirit is also wielded in the context of discipleship and teaching. As believers teach and disciple one another, they are equipping each other with the knowledge and application of God's Word. Paul instructed Timothy to "preach the word; be prepared in season and out of season; correct, rebuke and encourage—with great patience and careful instruction" (2 Timothy 4:2).

In discipleship, the sword of the Spirit is used to correct, guide, and encourage one another in the truth. This process of teaching and learning equips believers to wield the sword of the Spirit in their own lives and to pass it on to others.

3. Intercession and Spiritual Warfare:

The sword of the Spirit is also wielded collectively in intercession and spiritual warfare. When believers gather to pray, they can use Scripture as a powerful tool in their prayers. Whether praying for protection, healing, deliverance, or revival, declaring God's Word in prayer is a way of wielding the sword of the Spirit in unity.

The early church often prayed Scripture, as seen in Acts 4:24-31, where they prayed Psalm 2 in response to persecution. This collective wielding of the sword of the Spirit resulted in boldness and the advancement of the Gospel.

Conclusion: Wielding the Sword of the Spirit with Confidence

The sword of the Spirit, which is the Word of God, is a powerful and essential weapon in the life of every believer. It is the only offensive weapon in the armor of God, designed to defeat the enemy's lies, temptations, and attacks. As we have seen in the example of Jesus, Scripture is a potent tool for overcoming temptation and standing firm in the truth.

To wield the sword of the Spirit effectively, we must be diligent students of God's Word, hiding it in our hearts through study, meditation, and memorization. We must also be guided by the Holy Spirit, who gives us the wisdom and discernment to apply Scripture accurately and powerfully in our lives. Whether in personal spiritual battles, corporate worship, or collective intercession, the sword of the Spirit is our weapon of choice, capable of cutting through the darkness and bringing the light of truth.

As we go forth into the battles of life, let us take up the sword of the Spirit with confidence, knowing that God's Word is living and active, sharper than any double-edged sword. Let us declare His promises, stand on His truth, and wield His Word with boldness and authority. For it is the sword of the Spirit that will lead us to victory, enabling us to stand firm in the faith and to overcome the enemy by the power of God's Word.

Chapter 7: The Power of Prayer

Theme: The role of prayer in spiritual warfare.

Reflection: Discuss the importance of constant prayer in the life of a believer, particularly in the context of spiritual warfare. Reflect on how prayer strengthens the believer, provides guidance, and keeps us connected to God's power.

Prayer is the heartbeat of the Christian life, the lifeline that connects us with the Creator of the universe, and the most potent weapon we wield in spiritual warfare. Throughout Scripture, prayer is presented as an essential discipline, a means of communing with God, and a vital practice in the battle against spiritual forces. In the context of spiritual warfare, prayer is not merely a ritual or a religious exercise; it is a dynamic, powerful, and essential practice that fortifies the believer, provides divine guidance, and keeps us tethered to the inexhaustible power of God.

In this chapter, we will explore the critical role of prayer in spiritual warfare. We will delve into the ways prayer empowers and strengthens believers, examine how prayer provides direction and clarity in the midst of spiritual battles, and consider how prayer maintains our connection to God's power. Through reflection on biblical examples and practical applications, we will uncover the transformative power of prayer in the life of a believer.

The Foundation of Spiritual Warfare: Prayer as Connection with God

At its core, prayer is a means of communication with God. It is through prayer that we express our praise, thanksgiving, confession, and requests to God. But prayer is more than just communication; it is communion. It is the intimate fellowship between a believer and their Heavenly Father, where we not only speak to God but also listen to Him. This connection is vital, especially in the context of spiritual warfare, where the stakes are high, and the battles are fierce.

The Bible consistently emphasizes the importance of prayer as the foundation of spiritual warfare. In Ephesians 6:18, after describing the armor of God, Paul exhorts believers to "pray in the Spirit on all occasions with all kinds of prayers and requests. With this in mind, be alert and always keep on praying for all the Lord's people." This verse highlights the central role of prayer in the life of a believer, especially in the context of spiritual warfare. Paul's instruction to pray "on all occasions" underscores the necessity of constant, ongoing prayer as a means of staying connected to God and remaining vigilant against the enemy's schemes.

Prayer serves as the foundation of spiritual warfare because it keeps us connected to the source of our strength—God Himself. Without prayer, we are like soldiers cut off from their commander, lacking direction, support, and reinforcement. But through prayer, we remain in constant communication with our Commander-in-Chief, receiving His guidance, strength, and assurance in the midst of battle. Jesus Himself demonstrated this principle during His time on earth, often withdrawing to solitary places to pray (Luke 5:16). Even though He was the Son of God, Jesus recognized the importance of staying connected to the Father through prayer, especially during times of intense spiritual warfare.

In the Garden of Gethsemane, on the night before His crucifixion, Jesus prayed fervently as He faced the ultimate spiritual battle. Luke 22:44 tells us that "being in anguish, he prayed more earnestly, and his sweat was like drops of blood falling to the ground." In this moment of intense spiritual warfare, Jesus turned to prayer, seeking the Father's strength and submitting to His will. His example shows us that prayer is not just a last resort; it is the first line of defense and the foundation of our spiritual armor.

Prayer as a Source of Strength

One of the most profound aspects of prayer in the context of spiritual warfare is its ability to strengthen the believer. Spiritual warfare is not a battle fought with physical weapons or human strength; it is a battle that takes place in the spiritual realm, and it requires spiritual strength. This strength comes from God alone, and prayer is the means by which we access and appropriate His strength in our lives.

The Apostle Paul understood the importance of prayer as a source of strength in spiritual warfare. In Ephesians 6:10, he writes, "Finally, be strong in the Lord and in his mighty power." This command to be strong in the Lord is not an exhortation to rely on our own abilities but to draw strength from God's limitless power. Prayer is the conduit through which we receive this divine strength, enabling us to stand firm against the enemy's attacks.

In the Old Testament, we see numerous examples of how prayer served as a source of strength for God's people in the face of overwhelming odds. One such example is the story of King Hezekiah, who faced an imminent invasion by the Assyrian army. The Assyrian king, Sennacherib, had already conquered much of Judah and was now threatening Jerusalem. In his moment of desperation, Hezekiah turned to prayer. He went to the temple of the Lord and spread out the threatening letter from Sennacherib before God, praying earnestly for deliverance (2 Kings 19:14-19).

God heard Hezekiah's prayer and responded with a message of reassurance through the prophet Isaiah. That very night, the angel of the Lord went out and struck down 185,000 Assyrian soldiers, delivering Jerusalem from certain destruction (2 Kings 19:35). Hezekiah's prayer brought divine intervention, demonstrating the power of prayer to strengthen and deliver God's people in times of spiritual crisis.

Similarly, in the New Testament, we see the early church relying on prayer as a source of strength in the face of persecution. In Acts 4, after Peter and John were released from imprisonment and warned not to speak in the name of Jesus, they returned to the believers and reported what had happened. The church responded not with fear or retreat, but with prayer. They prayed for boldness to continue proclaiming the Gospel, even in the face of opposition (Acts 4:23-31).

God answered their prayer by filling them with the Holy Spirit and empowering them to speak the word of God with boldness. The place where they were gathered was shaken, and they were strengthened to continue their mission despite the threats against them. This account illustrates the principle that prayer not only brings divine strength to individual believers but also to the collective body of Christ.

Prayer as a source of strength is not limited to moments of crisis; it is essential for daily spiritual vitality. Just as a soldier must eat and rest to maintain physical strength, a believer must engage in regular prayer to maintain spiritual strength. Prayer renews our minds, refreshes our spirits, and equips us to face the challenges of each day with confidence and courage.

Prayer as Guidance and Clarity in Spiritual Warfare

Another critical role of prayer in spiritual warfare is providing guidance and clarity. The spiritual realm is complex, and the enemy's tactics are often subtle and deceptive. Without divine guidance, we can easily be led astray or become entangled in the enemy's snares. Prayer is the means by which we seek God's direction, discern His will, and navigate the spiritual battles we face.

In Proverbs 3:5-6, we are instructed to "trust in the Lord with all your heart and lean not on your own understanding; in all your ways submit to him, and he will make your paths straight." This verse underscores the importance of seeking God's guidance rather than relying on our own understanding. In spiritual warfare, our own wisdom is insufficient; we need the wisdom and direction that comes from God alone. Prayer is the vehicle through which we submit our ways to God and receive His guidance.

The Bible provides numerous examples of how prayer brought divine guidance and clarity in the midst of spiritual warfare. One such example is the story of Jehoshaphat, the king of Judah, who faced a massive coalition of enemy forces. In 2 Chronicles 20, we read that a vast army from Moab, Ammon, and Mount Seir came to wage war against Judah. Jehoshaphat was alarmed, but instead of panicking, he called the people of Judah to seek the Lord through prayer and fasting.

Jehoshaphat stood before the assembly of Judah and Jerusalem in the temple of the Lord and prayed, acknowledging their powerlessness and seeking God's intervention. He declared, "We do not know what to do, but our eyes are on you" (2 Chronicles 20:12). In response to their prayer, the Spirit of the Lord came upon Jahaziel, a Levite, who delivered a prophetic word of guidance: "Do not be afraid or discouraged because of this vast army. For the battle is not yours, but God's" (2 Chronicles 20:15).

God instructed Jehoshaphat and the people of Judah to march out against the enemy, but they were not to fight in the traditional sense. Instead, they were to take up their positions, stand firm, and see the deliverance the Lord would bring. The next day, as they went out to meet the enemy, Jehoshaphat appointed men to sing to the Lord and praise Him for the splendor of His holiness. As they began to sing and praise, the Lord set ambushes against the enemy forces, and they were defeated without Judah having to lift a sword (2 Chronicles 20:21-24).

This story demonstrates the power of prayer to bring divine guidance and clarity in the midst of overwhelming circumstances. By seeking God's direction, Jehoshaphat and the people of Judah were able to discern God's strategy for victory, which was completely unconventional by human standards. Their victory was won not by military might, but by obedience to God's guidance and the power of prayer.

Similarly, in the New Testament, we see the early church relying on prayer for guidance in critical decisions. In Acts 13, while the church in Antioch was worshiping the Lord and fasting, the Holy Spirit spoke to them, saying, "Set apart for me Barnabas and Saul for the work to which I have called them" (Acts 13:2). In response to this divine direction, the church laid hands on Barnabas and Saul (Paul) and sent them off on their missionary journey. This moment of prayerful discernment led to the expansion of the Gospel to the Gentile world and the establishment of numerous churches.

These examples underscore the importance of prayer as a means of seeking God's guidance and clarity in spiritual warfare. When we face difficult decisions, uncertain situations, or spiritual opposition, prayer is the key to discerning God's will and receiving His direction. By staying in constant communication with God through prayer, we are better equipped to navigate the complexities of spiritual warfare and to follow His lead in every situation.

The Power of Persistent and Faithful Prayer

One of the most significant aspects of prayer in spiritual warfare is persistence. The Bible teaches us the importance of persevering in prayer, even when we do not see immediate results. Persistent prayer demonstrates our faith in God's promises and our dependence on His timing and sovereignty.

Jesus emphasized the importance of persistent prayer in several of His teachings. In Luke 18:1-8, He told the parable of the persistent widow who kept coming to a judge, pleading for justice against her adversary. Although the judge was initially unwilling, he eventually granted her request because of her persistence. Jesus concluded the parable by saying, "And will not God bring about justice for his chosen ones, who cry out to him day and night? Will he keep putting them off? I tell you, he will see that they get justice, and quickly" (Luke 18:7-8).

This parable illustrates the power of persistent prayer in spiritual warfare. The widow's persistence in seeking justice is a model for believers to persist in prayer, especially when facing opposition from the enemy. God is not like the unjust judge; He is a loving and just Father who hears the cries of His children and responds to their needs. However, He may choose to answer in His own timing and according to His greater purposes. Our role is to remain faithful in prayer, trusting that God is working even when we cannot see it.

Another example of persistent prayer is found in the life of Daniel. In Daniel 10, we read that Daniel prayed and fasted for three weeks, seeking understanding of a vision he had received. During this time, Daniel received no immediate answer, but he continued to pray and seek the Lord. Finally, after 21 days, an angel appeared to Daniel and explained that his prayer had been heard from the first day, but the angel had been delayed by spiritual opposition from the prince of the Persian kingdom (a demonic force) (Daniel 10:12-13).

This account reveals that there is often spiritual resistance to our prayers, and the answers may be delayed because of spiritual warfare in the heavenly realms. However, Daniel's persistence in prayer eventually broke through the opposition, and he received the revelation he sought. This story encourages us to persevere in prayer, even when we face delays or obstacles, knowing that our prayers are powerful and effective in the spiritual realm.

Persistent prayer is not just about repeating the same requests; it is about maintaining a posture of faith, trust, and dependence on God. It is about continuing to seek God's will and to align our hearts with His purposes, even when we do not see immediate results. Persistent prayer is a demonstration of our faith in God's character and His promises, and it is a powerful weapon in spiritual warfare.

The Role of Intercessory Prayer in Spiritual Warfare

Intercessory prayer is a vital aspect of spiritual warfare, as it involves praying on behalf of others—whether individuals, groups, or nations. In intercessory prayer, we stand in the gap for those who may be unable or unaware of the spiritual battles they face. Through intercession, we partner with God in His redemptive work, bringing His power and presence into the lives of others.

The Bible is filled with examples of intercessory prayer in spiritual warfare. One of the most notable examples is found in the story of Moses interceding for the Israelites after they sinned by worshiping the golden calf. In Exodus 32, God's anger burned against the people, and He threatened to destroy them and start over with Moses. However, Moses interceded on behalf of the Israelites, pleading with God to relent from His anger and to remember His covenant with Abraham, Isaac, and Jacob.

Moses' intercession was so powerful that God relented from bringing disaster on His people (Exodus 32:14). This account demonstrates the power of intercessory prayer to change the course of events and to bring about God's mercy and grace in the midst of judgment. Moses' willingness to stand in the gap for the Israelites saved them from destruction and restored their relationship with God.

Another powerful example of intercessory prayer in spiritual warfare is found in the book of Daniel. In Daniel 9, we see Daniel interceding on behalf of the people of Israel, who were in exile because of their sin and rebellion against God. Daniel prayed a heartfelt prayer of confession and repentance, acknowledging the sins of the nation and pleading for God's mercy and forgiveness.

Daniel's prayer was so effective that the angel Gabriel was sent to him with a message of encouragement and insight. Gabriel revealed to Daniel the prophetic timeline of Israel's restoration and the coming of the Messiah (Daniel 9:20-27). Daniel's intercession not only brought about a response from heaven but also provided a revelation of God's redemptive plan for His people.

Intercessory prayer is a powerful weapon in spiritual warfare because it brings God's power and presence into situations where others may be unaware or unable to pray for themselves. It is an expression of love and compassion, as we lift up the needs of others before the throne of God. Intercessory prayer can break chains of bondage, bring healing and deliverance, and open the door for God's will to be done on earth as it is in heaven.

Prayer as Protection and Deliverance

Prayer is not only a weapon in spiritual warfare; it is also a means of protection and deliverance. The Bible teaches that God is our refuge and fortress, our shield and defender (Psalm 91). Through prayer, we seek God's protection over our lives, our families, and our communities, trusting in His power to deliver us from the schemes of the enemy.

One of the most well-known prayers for protection is found in Psalm 91, often referred to as the "Soldier's Psalm" or the "Psalm of Protection." This psalm speaks of God's protection over those who dwell in the secret place of the Most High, promising that He will deliver them from the snare of the fowler, the deadly pestilence, and the terror of the night. Psalm 91:4 declares, "He will cover you with his feathers, and under his wings you will find refuge; his faithfulness will be your shield and rampart."

This psalm is a powerful reminder that God is our protector, and through prayer, we can seek His covering and deliverance in times of danger or spiritual attack. Praying Psalm 91 over ourselves, our families, and our communities is a way of invoking God's protection and declaring our trust in His ability to keep us safe.

The New Testament also provides examples of prayer as a means of protection and deliverance. In Acts 12, we read the story of Peter's miraculous escape from prison. King Herod had arrested Peter and intended to bring him to trial after the Passover. While Peter was in prison, the church was earnestly praying to God for him (Acts 12:5). In response to their prayers, an angel of the Lord appeared in the prison, and Peter's chains fell off. The angel led Peter out of the prison, past the guards, and through the iron gate, which opened by itself. Peter was delivered from what seemed like certain death because of the fervent prayers of the church.

This account illustrates the power of prayer to bring about divine intervention and deliverance in the midst of spiritual warfare. The church's intercession for Peter resulted in a miraculous escape, demonstrating that God hears and answers the prayers of His people, even in the most desperate situations.

Prayer as protection and deliverance is not limited to physical threats; it also applies to spiritual dangers. In Matthew 6:13, Jesus taught His disciples to pray, "And lead us not into temptation, but deliver us from the evil one." This petition in the Lord's Prayer reminds us that we are in constant need of God's protection from the temptations and traps of the enemy. By praying for deliverance from the evil one, we acknowledge our dependence on God's power to keep us safe and to guide us away from the snares of the devil.

The Role of Prayer in Corporate Worship and Spiritual Warfare

While individual prayer is essential in spiritual warfare, there is also a significant role for corporate prayer within the body of Christ. Corporate prayer involves believers coming together to pray in unity, seeking God's will and interceding for one another. In the context of spiritual warfare, corporate prayer is a powerful expression of the church's unity and strength, as believers join together to seek God's intervention and to stand against the forces of darkness.

The early church provides a powerful example of the role of corporate prayer in spiritual warfare. In Acts 4:23-31, after Peter and John were released from imprisonment, they returned to the believers and reported what had happened. The response of the church was to come together in prayer. They lifted their voices in unison, acknowledging God's sovereignty and asking for boldness to continue proclaiming the Gospel in the face of threats. The result of their corporate prayer was that the place where they were meeting was shaken, and they were all filled with the Holy Spirit and spoke the word of God boldly.

This account demonstrates the power of corporate prayer to strengthen the church and to bring about divine intervention. When believers pray together in unity, their prayers are amplified, and the power of God is released in greater measure. Corporate prayer also fosters a sense of community and mutual support, as believers encourage one another and bear one another's burdens through prayer.

Corporate prayer is particularly important in the context of spiritual warfare, as it unites the church in a common purpose and strengthens the collective witness of the body of Christ. When the church prays together, it becomes a formidable force against the powers of darkness. In Matthew 18:19-20, Jesus said, "Again, truly I tell you that if two of you on earth agree about anything they ask for, it will be done for them by my Father in heaven. For where two or three gather in my name, there am I with them."

This promise highlights the power of agreement in prayer. When believers come together in unity and agree in prayer, their petitions carry greater weight, and God's presence is manifested among them. Corporate prayer is a vital aspect of spiritual warfare, as it brings the church together to seek God's will, to intercede for the lost, and to stand against the enemy's attacks.

Conclusion: The Transformative Power of Prayer

Prayer is the most powerful weapon in the believer's arsenal in the battle against the forces of darkness. It is through prayer that we stay connected to God, receive His strength, discern His guidance, and experience His protection and deliverance. Whether we are praying individually or corporately, prayer is the key to victory in spiritual warfare.

The examples of prayer in Scripture, from the intercession of Moses to the persistent prayers of Daniel, to the corporate prayers of the early church, demonstrate the transformative power of prayer in the life of a believer. Prayer is not a passive activity; it is an active engagement with the living God, who hears and answers our prayers according to His will.

As believers, we are called to be people of prayer, constantly seeking God's face, interceding for others, and standing firm in the midst of spiritual battles. The power of prayer lies not in the eloquence of our words, but in the One to whom we pray—the Almighty God, who is able to do immeasurably more than all we ask or imagine, according to His power that is at work within us (Ephesians 3:20).

Let us, therefore, commit ourselves to a life of prayer, recognizing that it is through prayer that we access the power of God, that we are strengthened for the battle, and that we experience the victory that Christ has already won for us. As we pray, let us do so with confidence, knowing that our prayers are powerful and effective, and that through them, we are advancing the kingdom of God and pushing back the forces of darkness.

In the words of the Apostle Paul, "Pray in the Spirit on all occasions with all kinds of prayers and requests. With this in mind, be alert and always keep on praying for all the Lord's people" (Ephesians 6:18). This is the call to every believer—to be vigilant in prayer, to stand firm in the faith, and to wield the power of prayer in the ongoing battle of spiritual warfare. For it is through prayer that we are connected to the One who is our strength, our shield, and our deliverer—the Lord Almighty.

Chapter 8: The Importance of Vigilance

Theme: Staying alert in the spiritual battle.

Reflection: Reflect on the need to stay vigilant and watchful, recognizing that the enemy is always seeking to attack. Discuss practical ways to remain spiritually alert and ready to respond to spiritual threats.

In the realm of spiritual warfare, vigilance is not just an option; it is a necessity. The Apostle Peter offers a sobering warning in his first epistle: "Be alert and of sober mind. Your enemy the devil prowls around like a roaring lion looking for someone to devour. Resist him, standing firm in the faith" (1 Peter 5:8-9). This passage vividly illustrates the need for believers to stay vigilant, recognizing that the spiritual battle is ongoing and that the enemy is always on the prowl, seeking opportunities to attack.

Vigilance in the spiritual life involves more than just being aware of the enemy's existence; it requires a constant state of readiness, an acute awareness of the spiritual environment, and a proactive approach to defending oneself and others against spiritual threats. In this chapter, we will explore the importance of vigilance in the spiritual battle, reflecting on why it is necessary and discussing practical ways to cultivate and maintain spiritual alertness.

Understanding the Nature of the Enemy

To fully grasp the importance of vigilance, it is essential to understand the nature of the enemy we face. The Bible clearly identifies Satan and his demonic forces as the adversaries of God and His people. From the beginning, Satan has sought to oppose God's purposes, deceive humanity, and lead people away from the truth. Jesus referred to Satan as "a murderer from the beginning" and "the father of lies" (John 8:44), highlighting his destructive and deceptive nature.

The Bible presents Satan as a cunning and relentless adversary who employs a variety of tactics to accomplish his goals. In Genesis 3, we see the first instance of Satan's deceptive strategy in the Garden of Eden, where he successfully tempts Eve by distorting God's words and appealing to her desires. This pattern of deception continues throughout Scripture, as Satan seeks to lead people astray through lies, temptations, and half-truths.

In addition to deception, Satan uses other tactics such as accusation, temptation, and fear. Revelation 12:10 describes Satan as "the accuser of our brothers and sisters, who accuses them before our God day and night." This role of accuser is evident in the story of Job, where Satan challenges Job's faithfulness and integrity before God (Job 1:9-11). Satan also tempts believers to sin, as seen in the temptations of Jesus in the wilderness (Matthew 4:1-11). Fear is another weapon in Satan's arsenal, used to paralyze believers and prevent them from stepping out in faith.

The Bible also portrays Satan as a powerful adversary with significant influence in the world. Ephesians 2:2 refers to him as "the ruler of the kingdom of the air," indicating his authority over the present world system that is opposed to God. However, while Satan is powerful, he is not omnipotent. His power is limited by God's sovereignty, and his ultimate defeat is assured through the victory of Jesus Christ.

Understanding the nature of the enemy helps us to recognize the need for vigilance. Satan's tactics are subtle and deceptive, and he is constantly seeking opportunities to exploit weaknesses in our spiritual defenses. If we are not vigilant, we can easily fall prey to his schemes. Therefore, it is crucial for believers to stay alert and watchful, recognizing that the spiritual battle is real and that the enemy is actively working to undermine our faith and lead us away from God.

The Call to Spiritual Vigilance

Throughout Scripture, believers are repeatedly called to stay vigilant and watchful in their spiritual lives. This call to vigilance is not just a suggestion; it is a command that is essential for our spiritual survival and growth. Jesus Himself emphasized the importance of vigilance in several of His teachings and parables.

One of the most well-known parables that underscores the need for vigilance is the Parable of the Ten Virgins, found in Matthew 25:1-13. In this parable, Jesus compares the kingdom of heaven to ten virgins who took their lamps and went out to meet the bridegroom. Five of the virgins were wise and brought extra oil for their lamps, while the other five were foolish and did not. When the bridegroom was delayed, all ten virgins fell asleep. At midnight, a cry rang out that the bridegroom had arrived. The wise virgins were prepared and ready to meet him, but the foolish virgins were caught unprepared and were left behind.

The key lesson of this parable is found in Jesus' concluding words: "Therefore keep watch, because you do not know the day or the hour" (Matthew 25:13). The parable emphasizes the importance of being spiritually prepared and vigilant, as we do not know when Christ will return or when we will face critical moments in our spiritual journey. Vigilance involves being spiritually ready at all times, ensuring that our faith is active and our relationship with God is strong.

In another instance, Jesus warned His disciples to "watch and pray so that you will not fall into temptation. The spirit is willing, but the flesh is weak" (Matthew 26:41). This exhortation was given in the Garden of Gethsemane, just before Jesus' arrest. Despite Jesus' warning, the disciples fell asleep instead of keeping watch, and when the moment of testing came, they were unprepared. Peter, who had confidently declared his loyalty to Jesus, ended up denying Him three times because he had not heeded the call to vigilance.

The call to spiritual vigilance is also echoed in the writings of the apostles. Paul, in his letter to the Corinthians, urged believers to "be on your guard; stand firm in the faith; be courageous; be strong" (1 Corinthians 16:13). Similarly, in his letter to the Thessalonians, Paul encouraged the church to be "alert and self-controlled" as they await the return of the Lord (1 Thessalonians 5:6).

These passages highlight the necessity of vigilance in the Christian life. Spiritual vigilance is not just about avoiding sin; it is about being proactive in our faith, staying spiritually alert, and maintaining a close relationship with God. It involves recognizing the spiritual realities around us, being aware of the enemy's tactics, and responding with faith, prayer, and obedience.

Practical Ways to Stay Spiritually Vigilant

While the call to vigilance is clear, the question remains: How do we stay spiritually vigilant in our daily lives? In a world filled with distractions, temptations, and pressures, maintaining spiritual alertness can be challenging. However, there are practical steps we can take to cultivate and sustain a vigilant spirit.

1. Cultivate a Deep and Consistent Prayer Life:

Prayer is one of the most powerful tools we have for staying spiritually vigilant. Through prayer, we remain connected to God, seek His guidance, and receive His strength. A consistent prayer life helps us to stay attuned to the Holy Spirit's leading and to discern the spiritual battles we face. In Ephesians 6:18, Paul exhorts believers to "pray in the Spirit on all occasions with all kinds of prayers and requests." This call to continual prayer emphasizes the need for an ongoing dialogue with God, keeping us spiritually alert and ready to respond to any situation.

To cultivate a deep and consistent prayer life, it is helpful to set aside dedicated times for prayer each day. This could be in the morning, evening, or throughout the day, depending on your schedule. In addition to these set times, practice "praying without ceasing" (1 Thessalonians 5:17) by maintaining an attitude of prayer throughout the day, offering up short prayers and thoughts to God as you go about your activities.

2. Immerse Yourself in God's Word:

Scripture is the foundation of our spiritual vigilance. The Word of God provides the truth we need to counter the enemy's lies and deception. It equips us with wisdom and discernment, helping us to recognize spiritual threats and respond with faith. The psalmist declares, "Your word is a lamp for my feet, a light on my path" (Psalm 119:105). By immersing ourselves in God's Word, we are better equipped to navigate the spiritual landscape and to stay vigilant against the enemy's schemes.

Regular Bible reading, study, and meditation are essential practices for staying spiritually vigilant. Consider setting a daily Bible reading plan that allows you to systematically read through Scripture. In addition to reading, take time to meditate on specific passages, allowing the Holy Spirit to speak to you through the Word. Memorizing key verses can also be a powerful tool in spiritual warfare, as it enables you to recall and declare God's truth in moments of temptation or attack.

3. Maintain a Close Relationship with Other Believers:

Spiritual vigilance is not a solo endeavor; it is something we pursue in community with other believers. The Christian life is meant to be lived in fellowship, where we can encourage, support, and hold one another accountable. Hebrews 10:24-25 encourages us to "consider how we may spur one another on toward love and good deeds, not giving up meeting together, as some are in the habit of doing, but encouraging one another—and all the more as you see the Day approaching."

Being part of a local church or a small group provides a vital support system in your spiritual journey. Regular fellowship with other believers helps you to stay spiritually sharp, as you learn from one another, pray for each other, and grow together in faith. It also provides opportunities for mutual accountability, where you can be honest about your struggles and receive encouragement and prayer from others.

4. Practice Discernment and Guard Your Heart:

Discernment is a crucial aspect of spiritual vigilance. It involves the ability to distinguish between truth and error, right and wrong, and to recognize the subtle ways in which the enemy may seek to deceive or lead you astray. Proverbs 4:23 advises, "Above all else, guard your heart, for everything you do flows from it." Guarding your heart involves being intentional about what you allow into your mind and spirit—whether through media, relationships, or activities.

To practice discernment, it is important to regularly examine your thoughts, attitudes, and actions in light of God's Word. Ask the Holy Spirit to reveal any areas where you may be vulnerable to the enemy's influence, and take steps to protect your heart and mind. This may involve setting boundaries on what you watch or listen to, being selective about the company you keep, and avoiding situations or environments that could lead you into temptation.

5. Stay Humble and Dependent on God:

Pride and self-reliance are the enemies of spiritual vigilance. When we become complacent or overconfident in our own abilities, we open ourselves up to spiritual attacks. James 4:6 reminds us, "God opposes the proud but shows favor to the humble." Staying vigilant requires a posture of humility, recognizing that we are dependent on God's grace and strength for every aspect of our spiritual life.

Humility involves acknowledging your need for God and regularly submitting yourself to His will. It also means being open to correction and guidance from others, recognizing that you do not have all the answers. By staying humble, you remain teachable and receptive to the Holy Spirit's leading, which is essential for staying vigilant in the spiritual battle.

6. Be Watchful in Prayer and Fasting:

Fasting, coupled with prayer, is a powerful spiritual discipline that sharpens your spiritual senses and heightens your awareness of the spiritual realm. Fasting involves denying yourself physical sustenance for a period of time in order to focus more intently on God and seek His guidance and strength. Throughout Scripture, fasting is often associated with times of spiritual warfare, repentance, and seeking God's direction.

Jesus Himself fasted for forty days in the wilderness before beginning His public ministry, and it was during this time that He faced intense temptation from Satan (Matthew 4:1-11). By fasting, Jesus demonstrated His reliance on the Father and His commitment to fulfilling His mission. In the same way, fasting can help you to stay spiritually vigilant, as it humbles you before God and sharpens your focus on the things of the Spirit.

Consider incorporating regular fasting into your spiritual routine, whether it is a weekly fast, a monthly fast, or fasting during specific seasons of need or decision-making. As you fast, combine it with focused prayer, seeking God's guidance, strength, and protection in the spiritual battle.

7. Regularly Examine Your Life:

Part of staying vigilant is regularly examining your life to identify any areas of weakness, compromise, or spiritual drift. The Apostle Paul encouraged the Corinthians to "examine yourselves to see whether you are in the faith; test yourselves" (2 Corinthians 13:5). Regular self-examination helps you to stay spiritually grounded and to address any issues before they become major problems.

Take time periodically to reflect on your spiritual journey, your relationship with God, and your commitment to His Word and His ways. Are there areas where you have become complacent or where you have allowed sin to take root? Are there areas where you need to grow or make changes? By regularly examining your life in light of God's Word, you can stay vigilant and make the necessary adjustments to stay on course.

The Dangers of Spiritual Complacency

While vigilance is essential for spiritual survival and growth, the opposite—spiritual complacency—poses a significant danger. Complacency is a state of self-satisfaction or indifference, often accompanied by a lack of awareness or concern for potential dangers or challenges. In the spiritual life, complacency can lead to spiritual apathy, a weakened faith, and ultimately, vulnerability to the enemy's attacks.

One of the most vivid examples of spiritual complacency in Scripture is found in the church of Laodicea, one of the seven churches addressed in the book of Revelation. Jesus' message to the Laodicean church is a sobering warning against complacency: "I know your deeds, that you are neither cold nor hot. I wish you were either one or the other! So, because you are lukewarm—neither hot nor cold—I am about to spit you out of my mouth" (Revelation 3:15-16).

The Laodicean church had become complacent, self-satisfied, and indifferent to their spiritual condition. They believed they were rich and in need of nothing, yet Jesus exposed their true state: "You do not realize that you are wretched, pitiful, poor, blind and naked" (Revelation 3:17). Their complacency had blinded them to their spiritual poverty and left them vulnerable to the enemy's deceptions.

Jesus' call to the Laodicean church was a call to repentance and renewed vigilance: "Those whom I love I rebuke and discipline. So be earnest and repent" (Revelation 3:19). The message to Laodicea serves as a warning to all believers to guard against spiritual complacency and to stay vigilant in their walk with God.

The dangers of spiritual complacency are manifold. When we become complacent, we lose our sense of urgency and our passion for God. Our spiritual disciplines—such as prayer, Bible reading, and fellowship—may begin to wane, leaving us spiritually weak and vulnerable. We may also become more susceptible to temptation, as our spiritual defenses are lowered. Over time, complacency can lead to a drift away from God, resulting in spiritual stagnation or even apostasy.

To guard against complacency, it is important to cultivate a spirit of humility and dependence on God, recognizing that we are always in need of

His grace and guidance. Regular self-examination, as mentioned earlier, can help to identify areas where complacency may be creeping in. Additionally, staying connected to a vibrant Christian community can provide the encouragement and accountability needed to maintain spiritual fervor.

The Rewards of Spiritual Vigilance

While the dangers of complacency are significant, the rewards of spiritual vigilance are profound. Staying spiritually alert and watchful not only protects us from the enemy's attacks but also positions us to experience greater intimacy with God, deeper spiritual growth, and the fulfillment of our divine calling.

1. Protection from the Enemy:

One of the primary rewards of spiritual vigilance is protection from the enemy's schemes. When we stay alert and watchful, we are better equipped to recognize and resist the devil's tactics. James 4:7 encourages us, "Submit yourselves, then, to God. Resist the devil, and he will flee from you." Vigilance enables us to stand firm in our faith, resisting temptation, deception, and spiritual attacks.

Vigilance also helps us to avoid spiritual pitfalls and to stay on the path of righteousness. By staying connected to God through prayer and His Word, we receive the wisdom and discernment needed to navigate the challenges of life and to make decisions that align with His will.

2. Deeper Intimacy with God:

Another reward of spiritual vigilance is deeper intimacy with God. When we prioritize our relationship with Him and stay spiritually alert, we experience a greater awareness of His presence and guidance in our lives. Vigilance fosters a deeper reliance on God, as we continually seek His strength, wisdom, and direction.

Intimacy with God is cultivated through consistent spiritual disciplines such as prayer, worship, and Bible study. As we engage in these practices with a vigilant heart, we draw closer to God and experience the joy and peace that come from walking closely with Him.

3. Spiritual Growth and Maturity:

Spiritual vigilance also leads to growth and maturity in our faith. By staying alert and engaged in our spiritual journey, we develop the qualities of perseverance, endurance, and resilience. Trials and challenges, when faced with vigilance and faith, become opportunities for growth and refinement.

In James 1:2-4, we are encouraged to "consider it pure joy, my brothers and sisters, whenever you face trials of many kinds, because you know that the testing of your faith produces perseverance. Let perseverance finish its work so that you may be mature and complete, not lacking anything." Vigilance in the face of trials leads to spiritual maturity, as we learn to trust God more deeply and to rely on His strength.

4. Fulfillment of Divine Calling:

Finally, spiritual vigilance positions us to fulfill our divine calling and purpose. God has a unique plan for each of our lives, and staying spiritually alert helps us to discern and pursue that calling. Whether it is in our personal lives, our families, our workplaces, or our ministries, vigilance enables us to stay focused on God's mission and to seize the opportunities He places before us.

Paul exhorted Timothy to "fan into flame the gift of God, which is in you through the laying on of my hands" (2 Timothy 1:6). This call to vigilance reminds us that our spiritual gifts and callings must be actively nurtured and pursued. By staying vigilant, we remain open to the leading of the Holy Spirit and ready to step into the assignments God has for us.

Conclusion: The Lifelong Call to Vigilance

Spiritual vigilance is not a one-time effort; it is a lifelong commitment. The spiritual battle is ongoing, and the enemy is relentless in his pursuit of God's people. As believers, we are called to remain watchful, alert, and ready to respond to the challenges and opportunities that come our way.

Vigilance requires intentionality, discipline, and dependence on God. It involves cultivating a deep and consistent prayer life, immersing ourselves in God's Word, staying connected to other believers, practicing discernment, and guarding our hearts. It also involves being aware of the dangers of complacency and taking proactive steps to stay spiritually sharp.

The rewards of vigilance are profound. By staying spiritually alert, we protect ourselves from the enemy's attacks, grow in our relationship with God, mature in our faith, and fulfill our divine calling. Vigilance is not just about survival; it is about thriving in our walk with God and living out our faith with purpose and passion.

As we conclude this chapter, let us heed the words of Jesus in Luke 21:36: "Be always on the watch, and pray that you may be able to escape all that is about to happen, and that you may be able to stand before the Son of Man." This is the call to every believer—to stay vigilant, to stand firm in the faith, and to be ready for whatever lies ahead. For it is through vigilance that we remain strong in the Lord, equipped for the spiritual battle, and prepared for the day when we will stand before our Savior and King.

Chapter 9: Unity in the Body of Christ

Theme: The strength of the church in spiritual warfare.

Reflection: Examine how unity among believers strengthens the spiritual armor of the church. Reflect on the importance of supporting one another in prayer and encouragement as we face spiritual battles together.

In the grand scheme of spiritual warfare, the strength of an individual believer is significantly magnified when that believer is part of a united church body. Unity in the Body of Christ is not a mere ideal or a pleasant concept; it is a vital necessity for the church's effectiveness in spiritual warfare. As individual members of the church come together in unity, they form a powerful defense against the attacks of the enemy and create an environment where the presence and power of God are manifested in greater measure.

This chapter will explore the importance of unity within the Body of Christ, focusing on how such unity strengthens the church's collective spiritual armor. We will reflect on the biblical basis for unity, the role of the church in spiritual warfare, and practical ways to foster and maintain unity among believers. Additionally, we will examine the importance of supporting one another through prayer, encouragement, and mutual accountability as we face spiritual battles together.

The Biblical Basis for Unity

The call to unity among believers is a central theme throughout the New Testament. Jesus Himself prayed for the unity of His followers in His High Priestly Prayer, recorded in John 17. In this prayer, Jesus asked the Father that all believers "may be one, Father, just as you are in me and I am in you. May they also be in us so that the world may believe that you have sent me" (John 17:21). This prayer highlights the importance of unity not only for the church's internal strength but also as a testimony to the world of the truth of the Gospel.

The unity that Jesus prayed for is not simply an outward conformity or agreement on doctrinal points; it is a profound spiritual oneness that reflects the unity between the Father and the Son. This unity is rooted in the shared life of the Holy Spirit, who indwells all believers and binds them together as members of one body. The Apostle Paul emphasizes this in Ephesians 4:4-6, where he writes, "There is one body and one Spirit, just as you were called to one hope when you were called; one Lord, one faith, one baptism; one God and Father of all, who is over all and through all and in all."

Paul's emphasis on "one body" underscores the reality that, in Christ, we are not isolated individuals but members of a collective whole—the Body of Christ. This body is diverse, consisting of many members with different gifts, backgrounds, and functions, yet it is united by the Spirit and called to work together in harmony. In 1 Corinthians 12, Paul uses the analogy of the human body to illustrate this unity in diversity: "Just as a body, though one, has many parts, but all its many parts form one body, so it is with Christ" (1 Corinthians 12:12).

This unity is not just a spiritual reality; it has practical implications for how we live and relate to one another. Paul exhorts believers to "make every effort to keep the unity of the Spirit through the bond of peace" (Ephesians 4:3). This call to maintain unity requires intentionality, humility, and a commitment to live in love and harmony with one another. It means prioritizing the well-being of the community over individual preferences and being willing to work through conflicts and differences in a spirit of grace and forgiveness.

The biblical basis for unity is clear: it is God's will for His people to be united, reflecting His nature and purpose in the world. This unity is not just for the sake of harmony; it is a powerful weapon in the spiritual battle. When the church is united, it stands as a strong and impenetrable force against the enemy's attacks, and it becomes a beacon of light and hope to a watching world.

The Role of the Church in Spiritual Warfare

To understand the significance of unity in the Body of Christ, it is essential to recognize the role of the church in spiritual warfare. The church is not just a gathering of believers; it is the primary instrument through which God advances His kingdom and defeats the forces of darkness. Jesus declared that He would build His church and that "the gates of Hades will not overcome it"

(Matthew 16:18). This statement affirms the church's role as a victorious force in the spiritual battle.

The church's role in spiritual warfare is multifaceted. First, the church is called to be a community of worship and prayer. In worship, the church exalts God and declares His sovereignty over all things, including the spiritual forces of evil. Worship is a powerful act of spiritual warfare because it shifts the focus from the enemy's schemes to the greatness of God, reminding believers of His power and faithfulness. As the church worships together, it creates an atmosphere where the presence of God is manifested, and the enemy's influence is diminished.

Prayer is another critical aspect of the church's role in spiritual warfare. In Ephesians 6:18, Paul instructs believers to "pray in the Spirit on all occasions with all kinds of prayers and requests. With this in mind, be alert and always keep on praying for all the Lord's people." Corporate prayer is a powerful weapon in spiritual warfare because it unites believers in intercession, aligns their hearts with God's will, and invites His intervention in the battle. When the church prays together, it stands as a united front against the enemy, invoking God's protection, guidance, and power.

The church is also called to be a community of truth. In a world filled with lies and deception, the church is the "pillar and foundation of the truth" (1 Timothy 3:15). As the church proclaims the truth of the Gospel, it exposes the lies of the enemy and brings people into the light of God's truth. The unity of the church in its commitment to the truth is crucial for its effectiveness in spiritual warfare. A divided church, where truth is compromised or diluted, becomes vulnerable to the enemy's deceptions and loses its ability to stand firm.

Finally, the church is called to be a community of love. Jesus said that the world would know His disciples by their love for one another (John 13:35). This love is not just a sentimental feeling; it is a powerful force that binds believers together and strengthens them in the face of adversity. Love covers a multitude of sins (1 Peter 4:8), and it fosters an environment where forgiveness, reconciliation, and mutual support can flourish. In the context of spiritual warfare, love creates a protective shield around the church, preventing the enemy from gaining a foothold through division, bitterness, or unforgiveness.

The role of the church in spiritual warfare is essential and cannot be overstated. The church is God's chosen instrument to advance His kingdom, proclaim His truth, and defeat the forces of darkness. This role requires the church to be united, standing together in worship, prayer, truth, and love. When the church is united, it is strong and effective in fulfilling its mission and in overcoming the enemy.

The Power of Unity in Spiritual Warfare

Unity in the Body of Christ is not just a pleasant ideal; it is a source of tremendous power in spiritual warfare. When believers are united in purpose, love, and commitment to God's will, they create an environment where God's presence is manifested in greater measure and where the enemy's influence is diminished.

One of the most striking examples of the power of unity in spiritual warfare is found in the story of Joshua and the battle of Jericho. In Joshua 6, God gave Joshua specific instructions on how to conquer the city of Jericho. The Israelites were to march around the city once a day for six days, and on the seventh day, they were to march around the city seven times. After the seventh lap, the priests were to blow the trumpets, and the people were to shout. When they did this, the walls of Jericho collapsed, and the Israelites were able to take the city.

This story illustrates the power of unity and obedience in spiritual warfare. The Israelites followed God's instructions together, marching in unison and trusting in His promise. Their unity in purpose and action created the conditions for a miraculous victory. If they had been divided, questioning Joshua's leadership or refusing to participate, the outcome would have been very different. The power of their unity was evident in the walls of Jericho falling before them.

In the New Testament, the power of unity is also demonstrated in the early church. In Acts 2, we read that the believers "were all together in one place" on the day of Pentecost (Acts 2:1). This unity in gathering, prayer, and expectation created the environment for the outpouring of the Holy Spirit. The result was the birth of the church and the empowerment of the believers to carry out the Great Commission.

The unity of the early church continued to be a source of strength in the face of persecution and opposition. In Acts 4, after Peter and John were released from imprisonment, the believers gathered together in prayer. They prayed for boldness to continue preaching the Gospel despite the threats against them. The place where they were gathered was shaken, and they were all filled with the Holy Spirit and spoke the word of God boldly (Acts 4:31). The power of their unity in prayer and purpose resulted in greater boldness, empowerment, and growth for the church.

Unity in the Body of Christ is not just about maintaining harmony; it is about creating the conditions for God's power to be released in greater measure. When believers are united in prayer, worship, truth, and love, they create an atmosphere where God is pleased to dwell and where His power is made manifest. This unity becomes a formidable force against the enemy, as the church stands together, resisting his attacks and advancing the kingdom of God.

Supporting One Another in Prayer and Encouragement

One of the most practical expressions of unity in the Body of Christ is the support believers offer one another through prayer and encouragement. In the context of spiritual warfare, this support is essential for maintaining spiritual strength, resilience, and victory.

Prayer is one of the most powerful ways we can support one another in the spiritual battle. James 5:16 encourages us to "confess your sins to each other and pray for each other so that you may be healed. The prayer of a righteous person is powerful and effective." Praying for one another not only brings God's intervention into our situations but also strengthens the bonds of unity within the church. When we pray for each other, we acknowledge our mutual dependence on God and our responsibility to care for one another.

Intercessory prayer is particularly important in spiritual warfare. There are times when a fellow believer may be facing intense spiritual attacks, discouragement, or temptation. In these moments, our prayers can make a significant difference in their ability to stand firm. Paul frequently asked the churches to pray for him as he faced various challenges in his ministry. In Ephesians 6:19-20, he wrote, "Pray also for me, that whenever I speak, words may be given me so that I will fearlessly make known the mystery of the gospel, for which I am an ambassador in chains. Pray that I may declare it fearlessly, as I should."

Just as Paul relied on the prayers of his fellow believers, we too can rely on the prayers of others in times of spiritual warfare. Knowing that others are praying for us provides strength, comfort, and encouragement. It reminds us that we are not alone in the battle and that we have a community of believers standing with us.

In addition to prayer, encouragement is another vital way we can support one another in spiritual warfare. Encouragement involves speaking words of life, truth, and hope to one another, reminding each other of God's promises and faithfulness. The writer of Hebrews exhorts believers to "encourage one another daily, as long as it is called 'Today,' so that none of you may be hardened by sin's deceitfulness" (Hebrews 3:13).

Encouragement helps to guard against discouragement, which is one of the enemy's most effective weapons. When believers are discouraged, they are more susceptible to doubt, fear, and temptation. However, when we encourage one another, we help to strengthen each other's faith and resolve. Encouragement can take many forms, from a kind word or note to a Scripture verse shared at the right moment, to simply being present and listening to someone who is struggling.

Supporting one another through prayer and encouragement is a practical expression of the unity we are called to in the Body of Christ. It reflects the love and care that should characterize our relationships with one another and serves as a powerful defense against the enemy's attacks. When we stand together, supporting each other in these ways, we create a strong and resilient community that is able to withstand the pressures and challenges of spiritual warfare.

Practical Steps to Foster Unity in the Church

While the importance of unity in the Body of Christ is clear, achieving and maintaining unity can be challenging. The enemy often seeks to sow seeds of division, conflict, and discord within the church, knowing that a divided church is weakened and less effective in its mission. Therefore, it is essential to take intentional steps to foster and protect unity within the church.

1. Prioritize Love and Humility:

Love and humility are foundational to unity. Paul exhorts believers in Philippians 2:2-3, "Make my joy complete by being like-minded, having the same love, being one in spirit and of one mind. Do nothing out of selfish ambition or vain conceit. Rather, in humility value others above yourselves." Love and humility involve putting the needs and well-being of others above our own and being willing to lay down our rights and preferences for the sake of the community.

Practicing love and humility requires a conscious effort to resist pride, selfishness, and the desire for recognition or control. It involves being willing to listen to others, to consider their perspectives, and to seek reconciliation when conflicts arise. By prioritizing love and humility, we create an environment where unity can flourish and where the enemy's attempts to divide are thwarted.

2. Foster Open and Honest Communication:

Communication is key to maintaining unity. Misunderstandings, assumptions, and unspoken grievances can quickly lead to division if not addressed. Therefore, it is important to foster a culture of open and honest communication within the church. This means being willing to have difficult conversations, to ask for clarification when needed, and to address issues directly rather than allowing them to fester.

Ephesians 4:15 encourages believers to "speak the truth in love." This balance of truth and love is essential for healthy communication. It involves being honest and transparent while also being sensitive and considerate of others' feelings. When communication is open and honest, misunderstandings can be resolved, trust is built, and unity is strengthened.

3. Practice Forgiveness and Reconciliation:

Forgiveness is a crucial aspect of maintaining unity. In any community, there will be times when people hurt or offend one another, whether intentionally or unintentionally. The enemy often uses these offenses as a foothold to create division and bitterness. However, forgiveness breaks the power of offense and restores unity.

Paul instructs believers in Colossians 3:13, "Bear with each other and forgive one another if any of you has a grievance against someone. Forgive as the Lord forgave you." Forgiveness is not always easy, but it is essential for maintaining unity. It involves letting go of resentment, choosing to release the offender from the debt of their offense, and seeking reconciliation.

Reconciliation goes beyond forgiveness; it involves the restoration of relationships. Jesus taught that if we have an issue with a brother or sister, we should go to them and be reconciled (Matthew 5:23-24). Reconciliation requires humility, a willingness to listen, and a commitment to restoring the relationship. When forgiveness and reconciliation are practiced within the church, unity is preserved, and the enemy's attempts to divide are defeated.

4. Engage in Corporate Worship and Prayer:

Corporate worship and prayer are powerful ways to foster unity within the church. When believers come together to worship God and seek His face, they are united in purpose and focus. Worship shifts the focus from individual preferences and differences to the greatness of God, creating a sense of oneness among the congregation.

In Acts 2:42, we read that the early church "devoted themselves to the apostles' teaching and to fellowship, to the breaking of bread and to prayer." This devotion to communal worship, teaching, and prayer created a strong and united church that was able to withstand persecution and opposition. Engaging in corporate worship and prayer helps to cultivate a spirit of unity and strengthens the bonds between believers.

5. Serve Together in Ministry:

Serving together in ministry is another practical way to foster unity within the church. When believers work together to fulfill the mission of the church, they develop a sense of camaraderie and shared purpose. Serving in ministry also allows believers to use their diverse gifts and talents to contribute to the common good, creating a sense of interdependence and mutual support.

In 1 Peter 4:10, we are instructed to "use whatever gift you have received to serve others, as faithful stewards of God's grace in its various forms." When believers serve together, they build relationships, develop trust, and strengthen the unity of the church. Serving together also helps to break down barriers of pride and self-centeredness, as believers focus on meeting the needs of others and advancing the kingdom of God.

6. Promote Unity in Diversity:

The Body of Christ is diverse, consisting of people from different backgrounds, cultures, and perspectives. This diversity is a strength, but it can also be a source of tension if not handled with care. Promoting unity in diversity involves valuing and celebrating the differences within the church while maintaining a commitment to the core truths of the Gospel.

Paul addresses the issue of diversity in 1 Corinthians 12, where he emphasizes that, while there are many different parts of the body, they all belong to the same body and are essential to its functioning. He writes, "But in fact God has placed the parts in the body, every one of them, just as he wanted them to be" (1 Corinthians 12:18). Promoting unity in diversity involves recognizing that every member of the church has a unique role to play and that diversity is part of God's design for the church.

Promoting unity in diversity also involves being intentional about creating an inclusive and welcoming environment where everyone feels valued and respected. This may involve addressing issues of prejudice, bias, or exclusion within the church and working to create a culture of openness and acceptance.

7. Remain Committed to the Mission:

Finally, unity in the Body of Christ is strengthened when believers remain committed to the mission of the church. The mission of the church is to make disciples of all nations, to proclaim the Gospel, and to advance the kingdom of God. When believers are united in their commitment to this mission, they are able to overcome differences and work together for the common good.

In Philippians 1:27, Paul encourages the church to "conduct yourselves in a manner worthy of the gospel of Christ. Then, whether I come and see you or only hear about you in my absence, I will know that you stand firm in the one Spirit, striving together as one for the faith of the gospel." This call to stand firm and strive together for the Gospel is a call to unity in mission. When the church is focused on its mission, it is less likely to be distracted by internal conflicts and divisions.

Conclusion: The Strength of Unity in the Body of Christ

Unity in the Body of Christ is not just a desirable quality; it is an essential component of the church's strength and effectiveness in spiritual warfare. When believers are united in love, purpose, and commitment to God's will, they form a powerful defense against the attacks of the enemy and create an environment where God's power is manifested in greater measure.

The Bible provides a clear and compelling vision of the importance of unity among believers. Jesus prayed for the unity of His followers, knowing that this unity would be a powerful testimony to the world and a source of strength in the spiritual battle. The apostles also emphasized the importance of unity, encouraging believers to prioritize love, humility, and mutual support.

The role of the church in spiritual warfare is significant, and this role requires the church to be united. Unity in worship, prayer, truth, and love creates a strong and resilient community that is able to withstand the pressures and challenges of spiritual warfare. The power of unity is evident in the biblical examples of the early church and in the stories of God's people throughout history.

Supporting one another in prayer and encouragement is a practical expression of unity that strengthens the church in the spiritual battle. When believers pray for each other and encourage one another, they build each other up and create a protective shield against the enemy's attacks.

Fostering and maintaining unity in the Body of Christ requires intentional effort and commitment. It involves prioritizing love and humility, fostering open and honest communication, practicing forgiveness and reconciliation, engaging in corporate worship and prayer, serving together in ministry, promoting unity in diversity, and remaining committed to the mission of the church.

As we conclude this chapter, let us remember the words of Psalm 133:1, "How good and pleasant it is when God's people live together in unity!" Unity in the Body of Christ is a source of joy, strength, and blessing. It is the foundation upon which the church stands in the spiritual battle and the means by which the church advances the kingdom of God. Let us, therefore, strive to maintain and promote unity in our churches, knowing that it is through unity that we experience the fullness of God's power and the victory that He has promised us.

Chapter 10: Standing Firm in the Faith

Theme: Perseverance in the face of spiritual opposition.

Reflection: Discuss the importance of standing firm in faith, even when facing intense spiritual opposition. Reflect on biblical examples of perseverance and how believers can cultivate this virtue in their own spiritual lives.

Perseverance is a fundamental aspect of the Christian life, particularly in the face of spiritual opposition. Throughout Scripture, believers are exhorted to stand firm in their faith, regardless of the challenges and trials they encounter. This call to perseverance is not merely about endurance; it is about holding fast to the truth of the Gospel, maintaining faith in God's promises, and continuing to live out our faith, even when circumstances are difficult and the opposition is intense.

In this chapter, we will explore the importance of standing firm in the faith, especially when confronted with spiritual opposition. We will reflect on biblical examples of perseverance, examining how these figures of faith remained steadfast despite the odds. Additionally, we will discuss practical ways believers can cultivate the virtue of perseverance in their own spiritual lives, enabling them to remain strong and faithful through every challenge.

The Call to Perseverance in Scripture

The Bible is replete with exhortations to persevere in the faith, recognizing that the Christian journey is fraught with challenges and opposition. Jesus Himself warned His disciples that they would face difficulties: "In this world, you will have trouble. But take heart! I have overcome the world" (John 16:33). This acknowledgment of the reality of trouble is coupled with the assurance of victory through Christ, which forms the foundation for the believer's perseverance.

The Apostle Paul, who faced immense opposition and suffering in his ministry, frequently emphasized the importance of standing firm in the faith. In 1 Corinthians 16:13, he exhorts the church, "Be on your guard; stand firm in the faith; be courageous; be strong." This command encapsulates the essence of perseverance—remaining vigilant, steadfast, and courageous in the face of opposition.

Similarly, in Ephesians 6:10-13, Paul uses the metaphor of spiritual armor to illustrate the need for perseverance in spiritual warfare: "Finally, be strong in the Lord and in his mighty power. Put on the full armor of God, so that you can take your stand against the devil's schemes. For our struggle is not against flesh and blood, but against the rulers, against the authorities, against the powers of this dark world and against the spiritual forces of evil in the heavenly realms. Therefore put on the full armor of God, so that when the day of evil comes, you may be able to stand your ground, and after you have done everything, to stand."

The repeated call to "stand" emphasizes the necessity of perseverance. The Christian life is not a passive existence but an active, ongoing engagement in spiritual warfare. To stand firm means to hold one's ground, to refuse to be moved or swayed by the pressures and temptations that arise. It is a determination to remain faithful to God and His Word, regardless of the external circumstances.

The writer of Hebrews also emphasizes the importance of perseverance, particularly in the context of faith. Hebrews 10:36-39 encourages believers to endure in the face of opposition: "You need to persevere so that when you have done the will of God, you will receive what he has promised. For, 'In just a little while, he who is coming will come and will not delay.' And, 'But my righteous one will live by faith. And I take no pleasure in the one who shrinks back.' But we do not belong to those who shrink back and are destroyed, but to those who have faith and are saved."

This passage highlights the connection between perseverance and the fulfillment of God's promises. Perseverance is not just about enduring hardship; it is about remaining faithful to God's will and continuing to live by faith, even when the fulfillment of His promises seems delayed. The assurance that "we do not belong to those who shrink back" serves as a powerful encouragement to press on in the faith, knowing that our ultimate reward is secure.

Biblical Examples of Perseverance

The Bible provides numerous examples of individuals who demonstrated remarkable perseverance in the face of intense spiritual opposition. These stories serve as powerful reminders that perseverance is not only possible but also rewarded by God. Let us examine a few of these examples and reflect on the lessons they offer for our own lives.

1. Job: Perseverance in Suffering

The story of Job is one of the most profound examples of perseverance in the face of suffering and spiritual opposition. Job was a righteous man who feared God and shunned evil (Job 1:1). Yet, despite his faithfulness, he experienced unimaginable suffering. In a short span of time, Job lost his wealth, his children, and his health. To make matters worse, his friends accused him of hidden sin, and his wife urged him to curse God and die (Job 2:9).

Despite these overwhelming trials, Job remained steadfast in his faith. He refused to curse God, even as he wrestled with deep grief, confusion, and despair. In Job 13:15, he declares, "Though he slay me, yet will I hope in him." This statement captures the essence of Job's perseverance—an unwavering trust in God, even when all evidence seemed to suggest that God had abandoned him.

Job's perseverance was ultimately rewarded. God vindicated Job, restored his fortunes, and blessed him with twice as much as he had before (Job 42:10-12). The story of Job reminds us that perseverance in suffering is not in vain. Even when we do not understand why we are facing trials, we can trust that God is sovereign and that He will bring about His purposes in our lives.

2. Joseph: Perseverance in Injustice

Joseph's life is another powerful example of perseverance, particularly in the face of injustice and betrayal. As a young man, Joseph was sold into slavery by his jealous brothers and taken to Egypt. There, he served faithfully in the house of Potiphar, only to be falsely accused of a crime and thrown into prison (Genesis 39).

Despite these injustices, Joseph remained faithful to God. In prison, he continued to serve with integrity, eventually gaining the favor of the prison warden. Even after interpreting the dreams of Pharaoh's cupbearer and baker,

Joseph was forgotten and remained in prison for two more years (Genesis 40:23; 41:1).

Yet, Joseph's perseverance paid off. God's timing was perfect, and when Pharaoh had a troubling dream, Joseph was brought before him to interpret it. As a result, Joseph was elevated to a position of power, becoming the second-in-command in Egypt. He was later reunited with his brothers, and in a profound act of forgiveness, he told them, "You intended to harm me, but God intended it for good to accomplish what is now being done, the saving of many lives" (Genesis 50:20).

Joseph's story teaches us that perseverance in the face of injustice is possible when we trust in God's sovereignty and His ability to bring good out of even the most difficult circumstances. Joseph's faithfulness, despite the long years of suffering and waiting, ultimately led to the fulfillment of God's plan for his life and the preservation of his family.

3. Moses: Perseverance in Leadership

Moses is another example of perseverance, particularly in the context of leadership. Called by God to lead the Israelites out of Egypt, Moses faced numerous challenges, including Pharaoh's stubbornness, the Israelites' constant complaints, and the hardships of the wilderness. Yet, despite these obstacles, Moses remained faithful to God's call.

One of the most significant tests of Moses' perseverance occurred at the Red Sea. With the Egyptian army pursuing them and the sea before them, the Israelites were terrified and cried out to Moses, questioning why he had brought them out of Egypt to die in the wilderness (Exodus 14:11-12). In this moment of crisis, Moses responded with faith and perseverance: "Do not be afraid. Stand firm and you will see the deliverance the Lord will bring you today" (Exodus 14:13).

God honored Moses' perseverance, parting the Red Sea and allowing the Israelites to cross on dry ground. Throughout his leadership, Moses continued to face challenges, from the rebellion of Korah to the Israelites' idolatry with the golden calf. Yet, he persevered, interceding for the people, seeking God's guidance, and leading them toward the Promised Land.

Moses' example reminds us that perseverance in leadership requires a deep trust in God's guidance and provision, as well as a willingness to endure challenges and opposition for the sake of fulfilling God's purposes.

4. Daniel: Perseverance in Faithfulness

Daniel's life provides a compelling example of perseverance in faithfulness, particularly in the face of opposition from powerful authorities. Taken into captivity in Babylon as a young man, Daniel remained faithful to God, even in a foreign land. His commitment to prayer and obedience to God's commands set him apart, earning him favor with the king but also making him a target for those who sought to undermine him.

One of the most well-known incidents in Daniel's life occurred when a decree was issued that no one was to pray to any god or man except the king for thirty days. Anyone who disobeyed would be thrown into the lions' den (Daniel 6:7-9). Despite this decree, Daniel continued to pray to God three times a day, as was his custom. His enemies seized this opportunity to accuse him, and Daniel was thrown into the lions' den.

Daniel's perseverance in faithfulness was rewarded by God, who sent an angel to shut the mouths of the lions, sparing Daniel's life. The king, witnessing God's deliverance, issued a decree that all in his kingdom should fear and reverence the God of Daniel (Daniel 6:26).

Daniel's story teaches us that perseverance in faithfulness, even in the face of life-threatening opposition, is possible when we prioritize our commitment to God above all else. Daniel's unwavering faith and perseverance not only preserved his life but also brought glory to God and influenced an entire kingdom.

5. Paul: Perseverance in Ministry

The Apostle Paul is one of the most remarkable examples of perseverance in ministry. Throughout his missionary journeys, Paul faced intense opposition, including beatings, imprisonment, shipwrecks, and persecution. Despite these hardships, Paul remained steadfast in his commitment to preach the Gospel and to strengthen the churches he had established.

In 2 Corinthians 11:23-28, Paul recounts the many trials he endured for the sake of the Gospel: "I have worked much harder, been in prison more frequently, been flogged more severely, and been exposed to death again and again. Five times I received from the Jews the forty lashes minus one. Three times I was beaten with rods, once I was pelted with stones, three times I was shipwrecked, I spent a night and a day in the open sea, I have been constantly on the move. I have been in danger from rivers, in danger from bandits, in danger from my fellow Jews, in danger from Gentiles; in danger in the city, in danger in the country, in danger at sea; and in danger from false believers. I have labored and toiled and have often gone without sleep; I have known hunger and thirst and have often gone without food; I have been cold and naked. Besides everything else, I face daily the pressure of my concern for all the churches."

Despite these overwhelming challenges, Paul's perseverance in ministry was driven by his deep love for Christ and his desire to see the Gospel proclaimed. He famously declared, "I consider my life worth nothing to me; my only aim is to finish the race and complete the task the Lord Jesus has given me—the task of testifying to the good news of God's grace" (Acts 20:24).

Paul's perseverance in ministry is a powerful example for all believers, particularly those who face challenges and opposition in their service to God. His life demonstrates that perseverance is fueled by a deep sense of purpose and a reliance on God's strength, even in the midst of suffering and adversity.

Cultivating Perseverance in Our Own Lives

Having reflected on these biblical examples of perseverance, the question arises: How can we cultivate this virtue in our own spiritual lives? Perseverance is not something that comes naturally; it requires intentional effort, discipline, and reliance on God's grace. Here are some practical ways to cultivate perseverance in the face of spiritual opposition.

1. Deepen Your Relationship with God:

Perseverance is rooted in a deep and abiding relationship with God. The more we know and love God, the more motivated we are to remain faithful to Him, even in the face of opposition. Cultivating a deeper relationship with God involves spending regular time in prayer, reading and meditating on His Word, and seeking His presence in worship.

In Psalm 63:1, David expresses his deep longing for God: "You, God, are my God, earnestly I seek you; I thirst for you, my whole being longs for you, in a dry and parched land where there is no water." This kind of deep, personal relationship with God is the foundation for perseverance. When we are rooted in God's love and presence, we are able to withstand the trials and challenges that come our way.

2. Renew Your Mind with God's Word:

The Word of God is a powerful source of strength and encouragement in the face of spiritual opposition. By regularly reading, studying, and meditating on Scripture, we renew our minds and reinforce our faith. The promises and truths found in God's Word serve as a firm foundation, enabling us to stand strong in the face of adversity.

Romans 12:2 exhorts believers, "Do not conform to the pattern of this world, but be transformed by the renewing of your mind. Then you will be able to test and approve what God's will is—his good, pleasing and perfect will." Renewing our minds with God's Word helps us to discern His will and to remain steadfast in our commitment to follow Him, even when the world around us is opposed to His ways.

3. Cultivate a Heart of Worship and Gratitude:

Worship and gratitude are powerful tools for cultivating perseverance. When we focus on worshiping God and giving thanks for His blessings, we shift our perspective from our difficulties to His greatness and faithfulness. Worship and gratitude help us to maintain a positive attitude and to remain hopeful, even in the midst of trials.

The Apostle Paul, who faced many challenges, was known for his attitude of worship and gratitude. In Philippians 4:4, he writes, "Rejoice in the Lord always. I will say it again: Rejoice!" This exhortation to rejoice is particularly powerful when we consider that Paul wrote these words while he was in prison. His ability to worship and give thanks, even in difficult circumstances, was a key factor in his perseverance.

4. Stay Connected to the Body of Christ:

Perseverance is not something we can cultivate in isolation; it requires the support and encouragement of other believers. Staying connected to the Body of Christ—through regular fellowship, corporate worship, and mutual accountability—is essential for maintaining perseverance in the faith.

Hebrews 10:24-25 emphasizes the importance of encouraging one another in the faith: "And let us consider how we may spur one another on toward love and good deeds, not giving up meeting together, as some are in the habit of doing, but encouraging one another—and all the more as you see the Day approaching." When we are connected to a community of believers, we are strengthened and encouraged to persevere, knowing that we are not alone in the spiritual battle.

5. Develop a Long-Term Perspective:

Perseverance requires a long-term perspective—a recognition that the Christian life is a marathon, not a sprint. This perspective helps us to endure temporary difficulties and to keep our focus on the eternal rewards that await us.

The writer of Hebrews encourages believers to run the race of faith with perseverance, fixing their eyes on Jesus: "Therefore, since we are surrounded by such a great cloud of witnesses, let us throw off everything that hinders and the sin that so easily entangles. And let us run with perseverance the race marked out for us, fixing our eyes on Jesus, the pioneer and perfecter of faith. For the joy set before him he endured the cross, scorning its shame, and sat down at the right hand of the throne of God" (Hebrews 12:1-2).

Developing a long-term perspective involves setting our minds on things above (Colossians 3:2) and remembering that our present sufferings are not worth comparing with the glory that will be revealed in us (Romans 8:18). This perspective enables us to endure hardships with patience and hope, knowing that our ultimate reward is secure in Christ.

6. Rely on the Power of the Holy Spirit:

Finally, perseverance is made possible through the power of the Holy Spirit working in us. The Holy Spirit is our Comforter, Counselor, and source of strength, enabling us to stand firm in the faith even when we feel weak or overwhelmed.

In Romans 8:26-27, Paul reminds us that the Holy Spirit helps us in our weakness: "In the same way, the Spirit helps us in our weakness. We do not know what we ought to pray for, but the Spirit himself intercedes for us through wordless groans. And he who searches our hearts knows the mind of the Spirit, because the Spirit intercedes for God's people in accordance with the will of God."

Relying on the Holy Spirit involves surrendering our own efforts and trusting in His strength and guidance. It also involves being sensitive to His leading, allowing Him to direct our steps and to empower us to persevere in the face of opposition.

The Rewards of Perseverance

While perseverance often involves enduring hardship and facing spiritual opposition, the Bible assures us that it is not without reward. The rewards of perseverance are both temporal and eternal, providing motivation and encouragement to remain steadfast in the faith.

1. Spiritual Growth and Maturity:

One of the immediate rewards of perseverance is spiritual growth and maturity. Trials and challenges, when faced with perseverance, have a refining effect on our character and faith. James 1:2-4 teaches that perseverance produces spiritual maturity: "Consider it pure joy, my brothers and sisters, whenever you face trials of many kinds, because you know that the testing of your faith produces perseverance. Let perseverance finish its work so that you may be mature and complete, not lacking anything."

Perseverance helps to develop qualities such as patience, endurance, and resilience. It deepens our trust in God and strengthens our ability to stand firm in the face of future challenges. As we persevere, we grow in our likeness to Christ and become more fully equipped to fulfill our God-given purpose.

2. Divine Protection and Provision:

Another reward of perseverance is experiencing God's protection and provision in the midst of trials. The Bible is full of promises that God will protect and provide for those who trust in Him and remain faithful. Psalm 91:14-16 declares, "Because he loves me, says the Lord, I will rescue him; I will protect him, for he acknowledges my name. He will call on me, and I will answer him; I will be with him in trouble, I will deliver him and honor him. With long life I will satisfy him and show him my salvation."

When we persevere in faith, we experience God's presence, protection, and provision in tangible ways. He sustains us through the trials and ensures that we have everything we need to remain faithful and victorious.

3. Eternal Rewards and Glory:

The ultimate reward of perseverance is the eternal glory that awaits us in the presence of God. The Bible repeatedly affirms that those who persevere to the end will receive a crown of life and the joy of eternal fellowship with Christ. In Revelation 2:10, Jesus encourages the church in Smyrna, "Be faithful, even to the point of death, and I will give you life as your victor's crown."

Paul also speaks of the eternal rewards that await those who persevere: "I have fought the good fight, I have finished the race, I have kept the faith. Now there is in store for me the crown of righteousness, which the Lord, the righteous Judge, will award to me on that day—and not only to me, but also to all who have longed for his appearing" (2 Timothy 4:7-8).

The promise of eternal rewards provides powerful motivation to remain steadfast in the faith, even in the face of the most intense opposition. Knowing that our perseverance will be rewarded with the joy of eternal life in God's presence gives us the strength to endure and to press on toward the goal.

Conclusion: Standing Firm in the Faith

Perseverance in the face of spiritual opposition is a vital aspect of the Christian life. It involves standing firm in the faith, holding fast to God's promises, and continuing to live out our faith, even when circumstances are difficult and the opposition is intense. The Bible provides numerous examples of individuals who demonstrated remarkable perseverance, reminding us that it is possible to remain steadfast, even in the most challenging situations.

As we seek to cultivate perseverance in our own lives, we can draw on the lessons from these biblical examples, as well as the practical steps of deepening our relationship with God, renewing our minds with His Word, cultivating a heart of worship and gratitude, staying connected to the Body of Christ, developing a long-term perspective, and relying on the power of the Holy Spirit.

The rewards of perseverance are both immediate and eternal. Perseverance leads to spiritual growth and maturity, divine protection and provision, and the joy of eternal fellowship with Christ. As we stand firm in the faith, we can trust that God will sustain us, empower us, and ultimately reward us for our faithfulness.

In the words of the Apostle Paul, "Therefore, my dear brothers and sisters, stand firm. Let nothing move you. Always give yourselves fully to the work of the Lord, because you know that your labor in the Lord is not in vain" (1 Corinthians 15:58). This is the call to every believer—to stand firm in the faith, to persevere in the face of spiritual opposition, and to trust in the God who is faithful to His promises. For it is through perseverance that we overcome, and it is through faith that we inherit the eternal rewards that God has prepared for us.

Chapter 11: The Role of the Holy Spirit

Theme: The Holy Spirit's guidance and empowerment in spiritual warfare.

Reflection: Explore the role of the Holy Spirit in guiding and empowering believers to effectively use the armor of God. Reflect on how the Holy Spirit equips us with wisdom, strength, and discernment in spiritual battles.

In the journey of faith, believers are called to engage in spiritual warfare, a battle not against flesh and blood, but against the rulers, authorities, and powers of this dark world and against the spiritual forces of evil in the heavenly realms (Ephesians 6:12). This battle requires more than human strength or wisdom; it demands divine empowerment, guidance, and discernment. Central to this empowerment is the Holy Spirit, the third person of the Trinity, who plays a crucial role in equipping believers to stand firm in the spiritual conflict.

The Holy Spirit is not merely an impersonal force or an abstract concept; He is a divine person who indwells believers, guiding, strengthening, and equipping them for the battles they face. In this chapter, we will explore the indispensable role of the Holy Spirit in spiritual warfare. We will examine how the Holy Spirit guides believers, empowers them to use the armor of God effectively, and equips them with wisdom, strength, and discernment. Through these reflections, we will gain a deeper understanding of how to rely on the Holy Spirit in our own spiritual battles.

The Holy Spirit: Our Divine Helper and Guide

Before delving into the specific ways the Holy Spirit aids in spiritual warfare, it is important to understand His nature and role as our divine helper and guide. Jesus, in His farewell discourse to the disciples, promised to send the Holy Spirit to be with them and to continue His work in their lives. In John 14:16-17, Jesus said, "And I will ask the Father, and he will give you another advocate to help you and be with you forever—the Spirit of truth. The world cannot accept him, because it neither sees him nor knows him. But you know him, for he lives with you and will be in you."

The term "advocate" (also translated as "helper" or "comforter") refers to one who comes alongside to offer support, guidance, and encouragement. The Holy Spirit is this advocate, sent by the Father at the request of the Son, to dwell within believers, guiding them into all truth and empowering them for the Christian life. The Holy Spirit is not a temporary visitor but a permanent resident within the believer, providing continuous guidance and support.

One of the primary roles of the Holy Spirit is to guide believers in the truth. Jesus declared that the Holy Spirit would "teach you all things and will remind you of everything I have said to you" (John 14:26). This guidance is not limited to theological understanding; it extends to every aspect of the believer's life, including the conduct of spiritual warfare. The Holy Spirit leads believers in understanding God's Word, applying it to their lives, and recognizing the truth in the midst of the enemy's lies and deceptions.

Moreover, the Holy Spirit provides believers with the wisdom and discernment needed to navigate the complexities of the spiritual battle. In 1 Corinthians 2:12, Paul writes, "What we have received is not the spirit of the world, but the Spirit who is from God, so that we may understand what God has freely given us." This understanding includes the ability to discern spiritual realities, to recognize the tactics of the enemy, and to respond with the wisdom that comes from God.

The Holy Spirit's role as our helper and guide is foundational to the believer's ability to engage in spiritual warfare. Without His guidance, believers would be vulnerable to the enemy's deceptions and powerless to stand firm. However, with the Holy Spirit's guidance, believers can navigate the spiritual battle with confidence, knowing that they are not alone but are led by the Spirit of truth.

Empowering Believers to Use the Armor of God

In Ephesians 6:10-18, Paul outlines the armor of God, a metaphorical representation of the spiritual resources available to believers as they engage in spiritual warfare. This armor includes the belt of truth, the breastplate of righteousness, the shoes of the gospel of peace, the shield of faith, the helmet of salvation, and the sword of the Spirit, which is the Word of God. While each piece of armor is crucial, it is the Holy Spirit who empowers believers to effectively use this armor in the battle against the forces of darkness.

1. The Belt of Truth:

The first piece of armor Paul mentions is the belt of truth. Truth is foundational to spiritual warfare, as it counters the lies and deceptions of the enemy. The Holy Spirit, who is the Spirit of truth, plays a vital role in equipping believers with this truth. In John 16:13, Jesus said, "But when he, the Spirit of truth, comes, he will guide you into all the truth." The Holy Spirit illuminates the truth of God's Word, helping believers to internalize it and to live in accordance with it.

Moreover, the Holy Spirit empowers believers to speak the truth in love, even in the face of opposition. In a world where truth is often distorted or suppressed, the Holy Spirit enables believers to stand firm in the truth and to bear witness to it, both in their words and in their actions.

2. The Breastplate of Righteousness:

The breastplate of righteousness protects the believer's heart and vital organs, symbolizing the righteousness that comes from God. This righteousness is not something believers can produce on their own; it is a gift from God, received through faith in Jesus Christ. The Holy Spirit is instrumental in applying this righteousness to the believer's life, enabling them to live in a way that reflects their new identity in Christ.

In Romans 8:10, Paul writes, "But if Christ is in you, then even though your body is subject to death because of sin, the Spirit gives life because of righteousness." The Holy Spirit empowers believers to live righteously, not by their own strength, but by the life-giving power of the Spirit. This righteousness guards the believer against the accusations and temptations of the enemy, enabling them to stand firm in their faith.

3. The Shoes of the Gospel of Peace:

The shoes of the gospel of peace equip believers to stand firm and to move forward in the spiritual battle. The gospel brings peace—peace with God, peace within, and peace with others. The Holy Spirit is the one who applies this peace to the believer's life and empowers them to walk in it. In Romans 8:6, Paul writes, "The mind governed by the flesh is death, but the mind governed by the Spirit is life and peace."

The Holy Spirit also empowers believers to share the gospel of peace with others. In Acts 1:8, Jesus promised, "But you will receive power when the Holy Spirit comes on you; and you will be my witnesses in Jerusalem, and in all Judea and Samaria, and to the ends of the earth." The Holy Spirit enables believers to proclaim the gospel with boldness, even in the face of opposition, and to bring the message of peace to a world in turmoil.

4. The Shield of Faith:

The shield of faith is designed to extinguish the flaming arrows of the evil one—arrows of doubt, fear, temptation, and accusation. Faith is not merely a mental assent to certain truths; it is a living trust in God and His promises. The Holy Spirit plays a crucial role in sustaining and strengthening the believer's faith.

In Galatians 5:22-23, Paul lists faithfulness as one of the fruits of the Spirit. This faithfulness is the result of the Holy Spirit's work in the believer's life, producing a steadfast trust in God, even in the face of trials. The Holy Spirit empowers believers to take up the shield of faith, enabling them to deflect the enemy's attacks and to stand firm in their trust in God.

5. The Helmet of Salvation:

The helmet of salvation protects the believer's mind, symbolizing the assurance of salvation in Christ. The Holy Spirit is the one who applies this assurance to the believer's heart and mind. In Romans 8:16, Paul writes, "The Spirit himself testifies with our spirit that we are God's children." This testimony of the Holy Spirit provides the believer with the confidence and assurance of their salvation, enabling them to stand firm in the face of doubt and fear.

The Holy Spirit also renews the believer's mind, transforming their thinking and aligning it with the truth of God's Word. In Romans 12:2, Paul exhorts believers to "be transformed by the renewing of your mind." This renewal is the work of the Holy Spirit, who enables believers to think rightly about God, themselves, and the world around them.

6. The Sword of the Spirit:

The sword of the Spirit is the Word of God, the only offensive weapon in the believer's armor. The Holy Spirit is the one who empowers believers to wield this sword effectively. In Ephesians 6:17, Paul explicitly identifies the sword of the Spirit as "the word of God." The Holy Spirit is the author of

Scripture, and He is also the one who brings it to life in the believer's heart and mind.

The Holy Spirit equips believers to use the Word of God in spiritual warfare, providing them with the right scriptures at the right time to counter the enemy's lies and attacks. Jesus Himself demonstrated this in His temptation in the wilderness, where He responded to each of Satan's temptations with Scripture (Matthew 4:1-11). The Holy Spirit empowers believers to do the same, enabling them to stand firm in the truth and to defeat the enemy with the Word of God.

The Holy Spirit's Role in Providing Wisdom and Discernment

One of the most critical aspects of spiritual warfare is the need for wisdom and discernment. The enemy's tactics are often subtle and deceptive, requiring believers to be vigilant and discerning. The Holy Spirit plays a vital role in providing the wisdom and discernment needed to navigate the complexities of the spiritual battle.

1. Wisdom for Decision-Making:

In the midst of spiritual warfare, believers are often faced with difficult decisions. These decisions may involve discerning the best course of action, identifying the source of a particular challenge, or determining how to respond to opposition. The Holy Spirit provides the wisdom needed to make these decisions.

James 1:5 promises, "If any of you lacks wisdom, you should ask God, who gives generously to all without finding fault, and it will be given to you." This wisdom is imparted by the Holy Spirit, who guides believers in understanding God's will and applying His Word to their specific situations. The Holy Spirit's wisdom enables believers to make decisions that are aligned with God's purposes and that lead to victory in the spiritual battle.

2. Discernment of Spirits:

Discernment is the ability to distinguish between different spirits—whether something is from God, from the enemy, or from the human spirit. This discernment is essential in spiritual warfare, as the enemy often disguises himself as an angel of light (2 Corinthians 11:14), making it difficult to recognize his schemes.

The Holy Spirit equips believers with the gift of discernment, enabling them to recognize the true nature of spiritual influences. In 1 Corinthians 12:10, Paul lists "the distinguishing between spirits" as one of the gifts of the Spirit. This gift allows believers to identify the presence and work of the Holy Spirit, as well as to detect the presence of demonic activity or deception.

Discernment is also essential for testing the spirits, as instructed in 1 John 4:1: "Dear friends, do not believe every spirit, but test the spirits to see whether they are from God, because many false prophets have gone out into the world." The Holy Spirit enables believers to test the spirits, to discern truth from error, and to avoid being led astray by false teachings or deceptive practices.

3. Guidance in Spiritual Warfare:

The Holy Spirit provides believers with guidance in the conduct of spiritual warfare. This guidance may come in the form of specific instructions, promptings, or insights that help believers to navigate the battle. The Holy Spirit may reveal strategies for prayer, insights into the enemy's tactics, or specific actions to take in response to a challenge.

In Acts 13:2-4, we see an example of the Holy Spirit's guidance in spiritual warfare. As the church in Antioch was worshiping and fasting, the Holy Spirit said, "Set apart for me Barnabas and Saul for the work to which I have called them." This guidance led to the commissioning of Paul and Barnabas for their missionary journey, which involved significant spiritual opposition but also resulted in the spread of the Gospel.

The Holy Spirit's guidance is essential for effective spiritual warfare. By relying on the Holy Spirit's leading, believers can avoid unnecessary pitfalls, make wise decisions, and engage in the battle with confidence, knowing that they are following God's direction.

The Holy Spirit's Role in Strengthening Believers

Spiritual warfare can be exhausting, both physically and spiritually. The constant opposition, trials, and challenges can lead to weariness and discouragement. In these moments, the Holy Spirit plays a crucial role in strengthening believers, renewing their energy, and enabling them to persevere in the battle.

1. Strengthening in Weakness:

The Holy Spirit strengthens believers in their moments of weakness. In Romans 8:26, Paul writes, "In the same way, the Spirit helps us in our weakness. We do not know what we ought to pray for, but the Spirit himself intercedes for us through wordless groans." This verse highlights the Holy Spirit's role in coming alongside believers, particularly when they are weak, discouraged, or unsure of how to pray.

The Holy Spirit's strength is made perfect in weakness, as Paul experienced in his own life. In 2 Corinthians 12:9-10, Paul recounts how the Lord responded to his plea for the removal of a thorn in his flesh: "But he said to me, 'My grace is sufficient for you, for my power is made perfect in weakness.' Therefore I will boast all the more gladly about my weaknesses, so that Christ's power may rest on me. That is why, for Christ's sake, I delight in weaknesses, in insults, in hardships, in persecutions, in difficulties. For when I am weak, then I am strong."

The Holy Spirit empowers believers to endure hardship, to face opposition with courage, and to persevere in their faith. This strength is not a result of human effort but is a manifestation of the Holy Spirit's power working within believers, enabling them to stand firm and to overcome.

2. Encouragement and Comfort:

The Holy Spirit is also known as the Comforter, providing encouragement and comfort to believers in times of distress. Spiritual warfare can be discouraging, particularly when the battle seems prolonged or when the desired outcome is delayed. In these moments, the Holy Spirit ministers to the believer's heart, reminding them of God's promises, providing peace, and renewing their hope.

In John 14:26-27, Jesus promised, "But the Advocate, the Holy Spirit, whom the Father will send in my name, will teach you all things and will remind you of everything I have said to you. Peace I leave with you; my peace I give you. I do not give to you as the world gives. Do not let your hearts be troubled and do not be afraid." The Holy Spirit's ministry of comfort and encouragement is vital for maintaining peace and hope in the midst of spiritual warfare.

The Holy Spirit also encourages believers through the Word of God, bringing to mind specific scriptures that provide comfort and assurance. This encouragement helps believers to keep their focus on God, to trust in His faithfulness, and to continue pressing forward in the battle.

3. Renewal of Strength:

In addition to providing strength in moments of weakness, the Holy Spirit renews the believer's strength, enabling them to persevere over the long term. Isaiah 40:31 promises, "But those who hope in the Lord will renew their strength. They will soar on wings like eagles; they will run and not grow weary, they will walk and not be faint."

This renewal of strength is the work of the Holy Spirit, who refreshes and revitalizes the believer's spirit. The Holy Spirit's renewal is not merely a temporary boost of energy; it is a deep, ongoing work that sustains believers through the challenges of spiritual warfare. As believers wait on the Lord and rely on the Holy Spirit, they experience a continual renewal of strength that enables them to run the race with endurance.

Cultivating Dependence on the Holy Spirit

Recognizing the indispensable role of the Holy Spirit in spiritual warfare, it is essential for believers to cultivate a deep dependence on the Holy Spirit in their daily lives. This dependence involves a conscious and intentional reliance on the Holy Spirit for guidance, strength, wisdom, and discernment. Here are some practical ways to cultivate this dependence:

1. Develop a Habit of Prayer:

Prayer is the primary means by which believers communicate with God and seek the guidance of the Holy Spirit. Developing a habit of regular, intentional prayer is essential for cultivating dependence on the Holy Spirit. In prayer, believers can seek the Holy Spirit's guidance for specific situations, ask for His strength in times of weakness, and invite Him to fill them with His wisdom and discernment.

In Romans 8:26-27, we are reminded that the Holy Spirit intercedes for us in our prayers, even when we do not know what to pray for. By cultivating a habit of prayer, believers remain connected to the Holy Spirit and are more attuned to His leading in their lives.

2. Immerse Yourself in God's Word:

The Holy Spirit works in conjunction with the Word of God, bringing it to life in the believer's heart and mind. Immersing oneself in Scripture is a crucial aspect of cultivating dependence on the Holy Spirit. As believers read, study, and meditate on God's Word, the Holy Spirit illuminates the truth, provides insight, and equips them with the knowledge needed for spiritual warfare.

Psalm 119:105 declares, "Your word is a lamp for my feet, a light on my path." The Holy Spirit uses the Word of God to guide believers, to renew their minds, and to equip them for every good work. By immersing themselves in Scripture, believers are better positioned to hear the Holy Spirit's voice and to follow His leading.

3. Cultivate a Sensitivity to the Holy Spirit's Promptings:

The Holy Spirit often leads and guides believers through promptings—subtle impressions, nudges, or thoughts that direct them in a particular way. Cultivating a sensitivity to these promptings involves being attentive to the Holy Spirit's voice and being willing to respond in obedience.

In Acts 8:29, we see an example of the Holy Spirit's prompting when He instructed Philip to approach the chariot of the Ethiopian eunuch: "The Spirit told Philip, 'Go to that chariot and stay near it.'" Philip's sensitivity to the Holy Spirit's prompting led to a divine appointment and the eunuch's conversion.

Believers can cultivate sensitivity to the Holy Spirit's promptings by spending time in quiet reflection, asking the Holy Spirit to speak to them, and being open to His leading. As believers practice responding to the Holy Spirit's promptings, they become more attuned to His voice and more confident in following His guidance.

4. Seek the Holy Spirit's Empowerment Daily:

Dependence on the Holy Spirit is not a one-time event; it is a daily necessity. Jesus instructed His disciples to wait for the Holy Spirit's empowerment before embarking on their mission (Acts 1:4-8). Similarly, believers need to seek the Holy Spirit's empowerment each day as they engage in the spiritual battle.

Ephesians 5:18 encourages believers to "be filled with the Spirit." This filling is an ongoing experience, where believers continually invite the Holy Spirit to fill them with His presence, power, and gifts. By seeking the Holy

Spirit's empowerment daily, believers are equipped to face the challenges of the day with the strength and wisdom that come from God.

5. Foster Community and Accountability:

Finally, cultivating dependence on the Holy Spirit involves fostering community and accountability with other believers. The Holy Spirit works not only in individuals but also in the community of believers. By engaging in fellowship, prayer, and worship with others, believers can encourage one another, share insights, and hold each other accountable in their walk with God.

In Acts 2:42-47, we see the early church devoted to fellowship, prayer, and the breaking of bread. This communal life was marked by the presence and power of the Holy Spirit, who worked in and through the believers as they supported one another in their faith. By fostering community and accountability, believers create an environment where the Holy Spirit can work powerfully and where they can grow in their dependence on Him.

Conclusion: The Holy Spirit—Our Source of Victory in Spiritual Warfare

The role of the Holy Spirit in spiritual warfare is indispensable. He is our divine helper, guide, and empowerer, equipping us with the wisdom, strength, and discernment needed to stand firm in the faith. Without the Holy Spirit, believers would be vulnerable to the enemy's attacks, unable to effectively wield the armor of God or to navigate the complexities of the spiritual battle.

As believers, we are called to cultivate a deep dependence on the Holy Spirit in our daily lives. This dependence involves a commitment to prayer, immersion in God's Word, sensitivity to the Holy Spirit's promptings, and a daily seeking of His empowerment. It also involves fostering community and accountability with other believers, recognizing that the Holy Spirit works powerfully in the body of Christ.

In the words of Zechariah 4:6, "Not by might nor by power, but by my Spirit, says the Lord Almighty." This declaration reminds us that the victory in spiritual warfare is not achieved through human effort or strength but through the power of the Holy Spirit. As we rely on the Holy Spirit, we are equipped to stand firm in the faith, to overcome the enemy's attacks, and to fulfill the purposes that God has for our lives.

Let us, therefore, commit ourselves to walking in step with the Holy Spirit, allowing Him to guide, empower, and equip us for the spiritual battle. As we do so, we can be confident that the Holy Spirit will lead us to victory, enabling us to stand firm in the faith and to bring glory to God through our lives.

Chapter 12: Overcoming the Flesh

Theme: The internal battle against sinful desires.

Reflection: Reflect on the internal aspect of spiritual warfare, focusing on the battle against the flesh and sinful desires. Discuss how the armor of God helps us overcome these internal struggles and live a life pleasing to God.

In the journey of faith, one of the most profound and ongoing battles believers face is the internal struggle against the flesh—the sinful nature that opposes the desires of the Spirit. This internal conflict is not merely a matter of human weakness or personal flaws; it is a fundamental aspect of spiritual warfare. The Apostle Paul describes this struggle vividly in his letters, highlighting the tension between the desires of the flesh and the leading of the Holy Spirit. Overcoming the flesh is essential for living a life that is pleasing to God, and it requires the full armor of God, empowered by the Holy Spirit, to achieve victory.

In this chapter, we will explore the nature of the battle against the flesh, examining how this internal conflict is a critical aspect of spiritual warfare. We will also discuss how the armor of God equips believers to overcome these internal struggles, enabling them to live in accordance with God's will. Through these reflections, we will gain a deeper understanding of how to navigate the internal battle against sinful desires and experience the transformative power of the Spirit in our lives.

The Nature of the Flesh and the Internal Battle

To understand the internal battle against the flesh, it is important first to define what the Bible means by "the flesh." In Scripture, the term "flesh" (Greek: *sarx*) often refers to the sinful nature inherent in all human beings due to the fall. This sinful nature is inclined toward self-centeredness, rebellion against God, and indulgence in sinful desires. The flesh is opposed to the Spirit of God and is the source of much of the internal conflict that believers experience.

The Apostle Paul provides a clear description of the nature of the flesh and the internal battle it creates in his letter to the Galatians: "For the flesh desires what is contrary to the Spirit, and the Spirit what is contrary to the flesh. They are in conflict with each other, so that you are not to do whatever you want" (Galatians 5:17). This verse highlights the inherent opposition between the flesh and the Spirit. The desires of the flesh pull us away from God and toward sin, while the desires of the Spirit draw us closer to God and toward righteousness.

Paul further elaborates on the works of the flesh in Galatians 5:19-21, listing behaviors and attitudes that are characteristic of the sinful nature: "The acts of the flesh are obvious: sexual immorality, impurity and debauchery; idolatry and witchcraft; hatred, discord, jealousy, fits of rage, selfish ambition, dissensions, factions and envy; drunkenness, orgies, and the like. I warn you, as I did before, that those who live like this will not inherit the kingdom of God."

These behaviors are manifestations of the flesh's influence in our lives, and they stand in stark contrast to the fruit of the Spirit, which Paul describes in the following verses: "But the fruit of the Spirit is love, joy, peace, forbearance, kindness, goodness, faithfulness, gentleness and self-control. Against such things there is no law" (Galatians 5:22-23).

The internal battle against the flesh is a daily reality for believers. It is not a one-time struggle but an ongoing conflict that requires vigilance, discipline, and reliance on the Holy Spirit. The flesh continually seeks to assert its dominance, tempting us to indulge in sinful desires and to live according to our own selfish impulses. However, as believers, we are called to live by the Spirit and to put to death the deeds of the flesh.

The Role of the Holy Spirit in Overcoming the Flesh

While the battle against the flesh is a formidable one, believers are not left to fight it alone. The Holy Spirit, who indwells every believer, plays a crucial role in empowering us to overcome the flesh and to live in accordance with God's will. The presence and power of the Holy Spirit are essential for victory in this internal battle.

1. The Indwelling of the Holy Spirit:

When a person places their faith in Jesus Christ, the Holy Spirit takes up residence within them. This indwelling of the Holy Spirit is a transformative experience that marks the beginning of a new life in Christ. The Holy Spirit regenerates the believer, giving them a new heart and new desires that are aligned with God's will.

In Romans 8:9, Paul writes, "You, however, are not in the realm of the flesh but are in the realm of the Spirit, if indeed the Spirit of God lives in you. And if anyone does not have the Spirit of Christ, they do not belong to Christ." The indwelling of the Holy Spirit signifies that the believer is no longer controlled by the flesh but is now under the influence of the Spirit. This new reality changes the dynamics of the internal battle, as the believer is no longer a slave to sin but is empowered to live in righteousness.

2. The Empowerment of the Holy Spirit:

The Holy Spirit not only indwells the believer but also empowers them to overcome the flesh. This empowerment is a dynamic and ongoing process, where the Holy Spirit provides the strength, wisdom, and guidance needed to resist the temptations of the flesh and to walk in obedience to God.

In Romans 8:13, Paul emphasizes the role of the Holy Spirit in putting to death the deeds of the flesh: "For if you live according to the flesh, you will die; but if by the Spirit you put to death the misdeeds of the body, you will live." The phrase "by the Spirit" indicates that it is through the power of the Holy Spirit that believers can mortify, or put to death, the sinful desires and actions that arise from the flesh.

This empowerment is not something believers can achieve through their own efforts; it is the result of the Holy Spirit's work in their lives. As believers yield to the Holy Spirit and seek His guidance, they are strengthened to resist the flesh and to live in a way that pleases God.

3. The Leading of the Holy Spirit:

The Holy Spirit also leads believers in their daily walk, guiding them away from the desires of the flesh and toward the things of God. In Galatians 5:16, Paul instructs believers, "So I say, walk by the Spirit, and you will not gratify the desires of the flesh." Walking by the Spirit involves living in step with the Holy Spirit's leading, allowing Him to direct our thoughts, attitudes, and actions.

The Holy Spirit's leading is a key aspect of overcoming the flesh. As believers submit to the Holy Spirit's guidance, they are able to discern the subtle temptations and deceptions of the flesh and to make choices that are in line with God's will. This leading of the Holy Spirit is a moment-by-moment process, requiring continual reliance on His presence and direction.

4. The Fruit of the Holy Spirit:

As believers yield to the Holy Spirit and allow Him to work in their lives, they begin to exhibit the fruit of the Spirit. This fruit stands in stark contrast to the works of the flesh and is evidence of the Holy Spirit's transformative power. The fruit of the Spirit—love, joy, peace, patience, kindness, goodness, faithfulness, gentleness, and self-control—reflects the character of Christ and serves as a powerful testimony to the Spirit's work within us.

The fruit of the Spirit is not something believers can produce on their own; it is the result of the Holy Spirit's indwelling presence. As believers cultivate their relationship with the Holy Spirit, they become more like Christ and less influenced by the desires of the flesh. The fruit of the Spirit serves as both a defense against the flesh and a means of living a life that is pleasing to God.

The Armor of God and Overcoming the Flesh

The armor of God, as described in Ephesians 6:10-18, is often associated with external spiritual warfare against the forces of darkness. However, this armor is also essential for the internal battle against the flesh. Each piece of the armor of God provides believers with the protection and resources needed to resist the sinful desires that arise from the flesh and to live in obedience to God.

1. The Belt of Truth:

The belt of truth is foundational to the armor of God, as it represents the truth of God's Word and the believer's commitment to live by that truth. In the internal battle against the flesh, the belt of truth serves as a defense against the lies and deceptions that the flesh may present. The flesh often seeks to justify sinful desires or to distort the truth in order to make sin appear more appealing.

By girding themselves with the belt of truth, believers are equipped to recognize and reject these lies. The truth of God's Word exposes the falsehoods of the flesh and provides a solid foundation upon which believers can stand. As Jesus declared in John 8:31-32, "If you hold to my teaching, you are really my disciples. Then you will know the truth, and the truth will set you free." The freedom that comes from knowing and living by the truth is a powerful weapon against the flesh.

2. The Breastplate of Righteousness:

The breastplate of righteousness protects the believer's heart, symbolizing the righteousness that comes from God and is imputed to believers through faith in Christ. In the battle against the flesh, the breastplate of righteousness serves as a shield against the accusations and temptations that the flesh may bring.

The flesh often seeks to exploit feelings of guilt, shame, or inadequacy, leading believers to either despair in their sin or to seek righteousness through their own efforts. However, the breastplate of righteousness reminds believers that their righteousness is not based on their own performance but on the finished work of Christ. This righteousness guards the believer's heart and enables them to stand firm in the face of the flesh's attacks.

Moreover, the breastplate of righteousness empowers believers to live righteously in their daily lives. As they rely on the Holy Spirit, they are able to resist the sinful desires of the flesh and to pursue a life of holiness and integrity.

3. The Shoes of the Gospel of Peace:

The shoes of the gospel of peace equip believers to stand firm and to move forward in their spiritual walk. The gospel brings peace—peace with God, peace within, and peace with others. In the battle against the flesh, the shoes of the gospel of peace provide stability and confidence, enabling believers to stand firm in the truth of the gospel and to resist the flesh's attempts to disrupt their peace.

The flesh often seeks to create turmoil, unrest, and anxiety, leading believers to act out of fear or insecurity. However, the peace that comes from the gospel anchors believers in the assurance of God's love and faithfulness. As Paul writes in Philippians 4:7, "And the peace of God, which transcends all understanding, will guard your hearts and your minds in Christ Jesus." This peace guards believers against the flesh's attempts to disturb their inner tranquility and to lead them into sin.

4. The Shield of Faith:

The shield of faith is designed to extinguish the flaming arrows of the evil one—arrows of doubt, fear, temptation, and accusation. In the internal battle against the flesh, the shield of faith serves as a defense against the flesh's attempts to undermine the believer's trust in God and His promises.

The flesh often tempts believers to doubt God's goodness, to question His promises, or to seek satisfaction in sinful desires rather than in God. However, the shield of faith enables believers to trust in God's character and to stand firm in His promises, even when the flesh is waging war against them. As Hebrews 11:1 defines faith, "Now faith is confidence in what we hope for and assurance about what we do not see." This confidence and assurance in God's faithfulness provide a strong defense against the flesh's attacks.

5. The Helmet of Salvation:

The helmet of salvation protects the believer's mind, symbolizing the assurance of salvation in Christ. In the battle against the flesh, the helmet of salvation serves as a defense against the flesh's attempts to sow seeds of doubt, fear, and confusion in the believer's mind.

The flesh often seeks to create confusion, leading believers to doubt their salvation, to question their identity in Christ, or to entertain thoughts that are contrary to God's will. However, the helmet of salvation reminds believers of their secure position in Christ and the certainty of their salvation. This assurance protects their minds and enables them to think rightly about themselves, God, and the world around them.

In addition, the helmet of salvation empowers believers to renew their minds and to resist the sinful thoughts and attitudes that arise from the flesh. As Paul exhorts in Romans 12:2, "Do not conform to the pattern of this world, but be transformed by the renewing of your mind." This renewal of the mind, empowered by the Holy Spirit, is a crucial aspect of overcoming the flesh.

6. The Sword of the Spirit:

The sword of the Spirit is the Word of God, the only offensive weapon in the believer's armor. In the internal battle against the flesh, the sword of the Spirit is a powerful tool for countering the flesh's temptations and lies.

The flesh often presents temptations that appeal to the believer's desires, emotions, or circumstances. However, the Word of God provides the truth that can cut through these temptations and reveal them for what they are. As the writer of Hebrews declares, "For the word of God is alive and active. Sharper than any double-edged sword, it penetrates even to dividing soul and spirit, joints and marrow; it judges the thoughts and attitudes of the heart" (Hebrews 4:12).

The Word of God exposes the flesh's deceitful desires and provides the believer with the wisdom and guidance needed to resist them. By wielding the sword of the Spirit, believers can effectively combat the flesh's attempts to lead them into sin and can stand firm in the truth of God's Word.

7. Prayer and Dependence on the Holy Spirit:

Finally, Paul emphasizes the importance of prayer in the context of spiritual warfare: "And pray in the Spirit on all occasions with all kinds of prayers and requests. With this in mind, be alert and always keep on praying for all the Lord's people" (Ephesians 6:18). Prayer is the means by which believers maintain their connection with God and their dependence on the Holy Spirit.

In the internal battle against the flesh, prayer is essential for seeking God's strength, guidance, and empowerment. Through prayer, believers can invite the Holy Spirit to fill them with His presence, to guide them in their decisions, and to empower them to overcome the flesh. Prayer also serves as a way to remain vigilant and alert, recognizing the subtle temptations and deceptions of the flesh and responding with spiritual discernment.

As believers pray in the Spirit, they are equipped to face the internal battle with confidence, knowing that they are not fighting alone but are empowered by the Holy Spirit to overcome the flesh and to live a life that is pleasing to God.

Practical Steps for Overcoming the Flesh

Overcoming the flesh is an ongoing process that requires intentionality, discipline, and reliance on the Holy Spirit. While the armor of God provides the necessary protection and resources, believers must also take practical steps to resist the flesh and to cultivate a life that is aligned with God's will. Here are some practical steps for overcoming the flesh:

1. Acknowledge the Reality of the Battle:

The first step in overcoming the flesh is to acknowledge the reality of the internal battle. This involves recognizing that the flesh is an active force that opposes the Spirit and that overcoming it requires vigilance and intentionality. By acknowledging the reality of the battle, believers can be more aware of the flesh's influence in their lives and can take proactive steps to resist it.

2. Cultivate a Life of Prayer:

Prayer is essential for overcoming the flesh. Through prayer, believers can seek God's strength, guidance, and empowerment to resist the sinful desires that arise from the flesh. Developing a habit of regular, intentional prayer helps believers to stay connected to God and to remain vigilant in the battle against the flesh.

In addition to personal prayer, it is also beneficial to engage in corporate prayer with other believers. Praying together provides mutual encouragement and accountability, and it invites the Holy Spirit to work powerfully in the community of believers.

3. Immerse Yourself in God's Word:

Immersing oneself in Scripture is a crucial aspect of overcoming the flesh. The Word of God provides the truth and wisdom needed to counter the flesh's temptations and lies. Regular reading, studying, and meditating on Scripture helps to renew the mind and to align the believer's thoughts and attitudes with God's will.

Memorizing key verses that address specific areas of struggle can also be a powerful tool in overcoming the flesh. When faced with temptation, believers can recall and declare these scriptures, using the sword of the Spirit to combat the flesh's influence.

4. Practice Self-Denial and Discipline:

Overcoming the flesh often requires self-denial and discipline. This involves saying "no" to the sinful desires of the flesh and choosing to live in obedience to God's Word. Jesus emphasized the importance of self-denial in discipleship: "Then he said to them all: 'Whoever wants to be my disciple must deny themselves and take up their cross daily and follow me'" (Luke 9:23).

Practicing self-denial may involve setting boundaries, avoiding situations that lead to temptation, and making intentional choices that reflect a commitment to holiness. Discipline is not about legalism or self-righteousness; it is about choosing to live in a way that honors God and resists the flesh's influence.

5. Stay Connected to the Body of Christ:

Overcoming the flesh is not something believers can do in isolation; it requires the support and encouragement of other believers. Staying connected to the Body of Christ—through regular fellowship, worship, and accountability—is essential for maintaining spiritual strength and for resisting the flesh.

Engaging in small groups, discipleship relationships, or accountability partnerships provides a safe space for believers to share their struggles, to receive prayer and encouragement, and to hold one another accountable in their walk with God.

6. Rely on the Power of the Holy Spirit:

Ultimately, overcoming the flesh is not something that can be achieved through human effort alone; it requires the power of the Holy Spirit. By cultivating a deep dependence on the Holy Spirit, believers can access the strength, wisdom, and guidance needed to resist the flesh and to live in accordance with God's will.

This dependence involves inviting the Holy Spirit to fill every area of the believer's life, to guide their decisions, and to empower them to overcome the flesh. As believers yield to the Holy Spirit, they experience His transformative power and are equipped to live a life that is pleasing to God.

The Rewards of Overcoming the Flesh

While the battle against the flesh is challenging, the rewards of overcoming the flesh are profound. These rewards include spiritual growth, increased intimacy with God, and the fulfillment of God's purposes in the believer's life.

1. Spiritual Growth and Maturity:

Overcoming the flesh leads to spiritual growth and maturity. As believers resist the sinful desires of the flesh and yield to the Holy Spirit, they become more like Christ and grow in their faith. This growth is reflected in the development of the fruit of the Spirit and in the deepening of the believer's relationship with God.

Spiritual growth also involves a greater capacity to discern and resist the flesh's influence, leading to increased victory in the internal battle. As believers mature in their faith, they become more effective in their witness to others and more fruitful in their ministry.

2. Increased Intimacy with God:

Overcoming the flesh leads to increased intimacy with God. As believers walk in obedience to God's Word and rely on the Holy Spirit, they experience a deeper connection with God and a greater awareness of His presence in their lives.

This intimacy with God brings a sense of peace, joy, and fulfillment that transcends the fleeting pleasures of sin. As believers draw closer to God, they experience the abundant life that Jesus promised: "I have come that they may have life, and have it to the full" (John 10:10).

3. Fulfillment of God's Purposes:

Overcoming the flesh enables believers to fulfill God's purposes in their lives. The flesh often seeks to hinder or derail the believer's pursuit of God's will, leading them into sin or distraction. However, as believers overcome the flesh, they are free to pursue God's calling and to walk in the good works that He has prepared for them.

The fulfillment of God's purposes brings a sense of meaning and purpose to the believer's life. It also results in the advancement of God's kingdom and the impact of the Gospel on others. As believers overcome the flesh and walk in obedience to God, they contribute to the fulfillment of His redemptive plan in the world.

Conclusion: Living in Victory Over the Flesh

The internal battle against the flesh is a significant aspect of spiritual warfare, requiring vigilance, discipline, and reliance on the Holy Spirit. While the flesh continually seeks to assert its influence, believers are not left to fight this battle alone. The Holy Spirit, who indwells and empowers believers, provides the strength, wisdom, and guidance needed to overcome the flesh and to live a life that is pleasing to God.

The armor of God, as described in Ephesians 6:10-18, is essential for overcoming the flesh. Each piece of armor equips believers with the protection and resources needed to resist the sinful desires that arise from the flesh and to stand firm in the truth of God's Word. By girding themselves with the belt of truth, donning the breastplate of righteousness, fitting their feet with the gospel of peace, taking up the shield of faith, wearing the helmet of salvation, and wielding the sword of the Spirit, believers are equipped to face the internal battle with confidence and to experience victory over the flesh.

As believers take practical steps to overcome the flesh—through prayer, immersion in God's Word, self-denial, fellowship with other believers, and reliance on the Holy Spirit—they experience the rewards of spiritual growth, increased intimacy with God, and the fulfillment of His purposes in their lives. These rewards are not only for this life but also for eternity, as believers walk in the abundant life that Jesus promised and contribute to the advancement of His kingdom.

In the words of the Apostle Paul, "So I say, walk by the Spirit, and you will not gratify the desires of the flesh" (Galatians 5:16). This is the call to every believer—to walk by the Spirit, to rely on His power and guidance, and to live in victory over the flesh. As we do so, we reflect the character of Christ, bring glory to God, and experience the fullness of life that He has prepared for us.

Chapter 13: Defeating the Powers of Darkness

Theme: Victory over demonic forces.

Reflection: Examine the believer's authority over demonic forces through Christ. Reflect on how the armor of God enables us to stand firm against these forces and claim victory in Jesus' name.

The reality of spiritual warfare is a constant in the life of a believer. This warfare is not only against the internal struggle with the flesh but also against external, malevolent forces—demonic powers that seek to undermine our faith and thwart God's purposes in our lives. Throughout Scripture, believers are called to stand firm against these powers of darkness, assured of their authority in Christ and equipped with the armor of God. The victory that Jesus Christ has secured over these demonic forces provides the foundation for our confidence and strength in spiritual warfare.

In this chapter, we will explore the believer's authority over demonic forces through Christ, examining how this authority is exercised in the context of spiritual warfare. We will also reflect on how the armor of God equips us to stand firm against these forces, enabling us to claim victory in Jesus' name. Through these reflections, we will gain a deeper understanding of the nature of our spiritual battle and the power that we possess as followers of Christ to defeat the powers of darkness.

Understanding the Powers of Darkness

Before delving into the believer's authority over demonic forces, it is important to understand the nature of these forces and their role in spiritual warfare. The Bible clearly teaches that there are spiritual beings—referred to as demons or unclean spirits—that are actively opposed to God and His people. These demonic forces operate under the leadership of Satan, the adversary of God, and they seek to carry out his agenda of deception, destruction, and rebellion against God.

1. The Nature of Demonic Forces:

Demonic forces are fallen angels who rebelled against God and were cast out of heaven along with Satan. These beings are intelligent, powerful, and malevolent, actively working to oppose God's purposes and to deceive humanity. In Ephesians 6:12, Paul describes the nature of our spiritual enemies: "For our struggle is not against flesh and blood, but against the rulers, against the authorities, against the powers of this dark world and against the spiritual forces of evil in the heavenly realms."

This verse highlights the organized and hierarchical nature of demonic forces. They operate under a structured system of rulers, authorities, and powers, each with specific roles and responsibilities in carrying out Satan's agenda. These forces of darkness are not merely passive or distant; they are actively engaged in spiritual warfare against believers, seeking to deceive, tempt, and oppress.

2. The Tactics of Demonic Forces:

The tactics of demonic forces are varied and subtle. One of their primary strategies is deception. Jesus described Satan as "a liar and the father of lies" (John 8:44), and this description applies to his demonic agents as well. Demonic forces often seek to distort the truth, leading people away from God's Word and into falsehood. This deception can take many forms, from false teachings and ideologies to personal temptations that appeal to the desires of the flesh.

Another tactic of demonic forces is temptation. Just as Satan tempted Jesus in the wilderness (Matthew 4:1-11), demonic forces seek to lure believers into sin by appealing to their weaknesses and desires. These temptations are designed to lead believers away from obedience to God and to ensnare them in patterns of sin and disobedience.

Oppression is another tactic used by demonic forces. This can manifest in various ways, including physical illness, mental and emotional distress, and spiritual heaviness. While not all suffering is directly caused by demonic forces, they often seek to exploit moments of weakness and vulnerability to bring about oppression and despair.

Finally, demonic forces may seek to instill fear and doubt in the hearts of believers. Fear is a powerful weapon in the enemy's arsenal, as it can paralyze believers, causing them to shrink back from their faith and to question God's goodness and power. Doubt is another tool used by demonic forces to undermine the believer's confidence in God's promises and to erode their faith.

3. The Limited Power of Demonic Forces:

While demonic forces are powerful and formidable, it is crucial to recognize that their power is limited. They are created beings, not equal to God, and they operate under the constraints of His sovereign will. The ultimate defeat of Satan and his demonic forces was secured by Jesus Christ through His death and resurrection. Colossians 2:15 declares, "And having disarmed the powers and authorities, he made a public spectacle of them, triumphing over them by the cross."

This victory means that while demonic forces continue to operate in the world, their ultimate defeat is assured, and their power over believers is limited by the authority of Christ. Believers, therefore, do not need to fear these forces, but can stand firm in the authority and victory that Christ has won.

The Believer's Authority Over Demonic Forces

The authority of believers over demonic forces is rooted in the victory of Jesus Christ. Through His death and resurrection, Jesus triumphed over the powers of darkness, disarming them and breaking their hold over humanity. This victory has been extended to all who believe in Him, granting them authority over demonic forces in His name.

1. The Victory of Jesus Christ:

The victory of Jesus Christ over demonic forces is a central theme in the New Testament. Throughout His earthly ministry, Jesus demonstrated His authority over demons by casting them out and setting people free from their oppression. In Matthew 12:28, Jesus declared, "But if it is by the Spirit of God that I drive out demons, then the kingdom of God has come upon you."

This statement underscores the reality that Jesus' authority over demonic forces is a manifestation of the kingdom of God breaking into the world. His victory over Satan and his demons was ultimately secured through His sacrificial death on the cross and His resurrection from the dead. In Hebrews 2:14-15, the writer explains, "Since the children have flesh and blood, he too shared in their humanity so that by his death he might break the power of him who holds the power of death—that is, the devil—and free those who all their lives were held in slavery by their fear of death."

Jesus' victory over Satan and demonic forces means that they no longer have ultimate power over those who belong to Christ. Believers are no longer enslaved to sin, fear, or the devil's schemes, but are set free to live in the light of God's truth and love.

2. The Authority of the Believer:

The authority that believers have over demonic forces is derived from their union with Christ. When a person places their faith in Jesus, they are united with Him in His death, burial, and resurrection. This union means that believers share in Christ's victory and are empowered to exercise His authority over demonic forces.

In Luke 10:19, Jesus imparted this authority to His disciples, saying, "I have given you authority to trample on snakes and scorpions and to overcome all the power of the enemy; nothing will harm you." This authority was not limited to the original disciples but extends to all who follow Christ. It is an authority that is exercised in His name, under His lordship, and according to His will.

The authority of the believer over demonic forces is not an inherent power that resides within the believer themselves; it is the delegated authority of Christ. This means that believers must always exercise this authority in submission to Christ and in reliance on the Holy Spirit. It also means that the authority is not to be used for selfish or manipulative purposes but for the advancement of God's kingdom and the deliverance of those who are oppressed by the enemy.

3. Exercising Authority in Spiritual Warfare:

Exercising authority over demonic forces involves both offensive and defensive strategies. Offensively, believers are called to resist the devil and to take a stand against his schemes. James 4:7 instructs, "Submit yourselves, then, to God. Resist the devil, and he will flee from you." This resistance is not passive but active, involving prayer, the declaration of God's Word, and the rejection of the devil's lies and temptations.

Defensively, believers are called to stand firm in the faith, putting on the full armor of God to withstand the attacks of the enemy. In Ephesians 6:11, Paul exhorts, "Put on the full armor of God, so that you can take your stand against the devil's schemes." The armor of God, as we will explore further, provides the necessary protection and resources for believers to stand firm against demonic forces and to claim victory in Jesus' name.

In both offensive and defensive strategies, the key is reliance on the power and authority of Christ. Believers must remain rooted in their identity in Christ, confident in His victory, and dependent on the Holy Spirit for guidance and strength.

The Armor of God and Victory Over Demonic Forces

The armor of God, described in Ephesians 6:10-18, is a vital resource for believers as they engage in spiritual warfare against demonic forces. This armor equips believers with the protection and tools needed to stand firm against the enemy and to claim victory in the name of Jesus.

1. The Belt of Truth:

The belt of truth is the first piece of armor mentioned by Paul, and it represents the foundational truth of God's Word. In the context of spiritual warfare, the belt of truth is essential for discerning and rejecting the lies and deceptions of demonic forces. Satan is the father of lies, and his demonic agents often seek to distort the truth, leading people away from God's Word and into falsehood.

By girding themselves with the belt of truth, believers are equipped to recognize and reject these lies. The truth of God's Word exposes the falsehoods of the enemy and provides a solid foundation upon which believers can stand. Jesus declared in John 8:32, "Then you will know the truth, and the truth will set you free." This freedom from deception is a powerful weapon in the battle against demonic forces.

The belt of truth also involves a commitment to living in truthfulness and integrity. Demonic forces thrive in environments of deception, hypocrisy, and hidden sin. By walking in the light of truth, believers deny the enemy a foothold in their lives and create a barrier against his attacks.

2. The Breastplate of Righteousness:

The breastplate of righteousness protects the believer's heart, symbolizing the righteousness that comes from God and is imputed to believers through faith in Christ. In spiritual warfare, the breastplate of righteousness serves as a shield against the accusations and temptations of demonic forces.

Satan is known as the accuser of the brethren (Revelation 12:10), and his demonic agents often seek to undermine the believer's confidence by reminding them of their past sins, failures, and shortcomings. The breastplate of righteousness protects the believer from these accusations, reminding them that their righteousness is not based on their own performance but on the finished work of Christ.

This righteousness also empowers believers to live righteously in their daily lives. By relying on the Holy Spirit, they are able to resist the temptations of the enemy and to pursue a life of holiness and integrity. This righteous living serves as a powerful testimony to the world and a defense against the attacks of demonic forces.

3. The Shoes of the Gospel of Peace:

The shoes of the gospel of peace equip believers to stand firm and to move forward in their spiritual walk. The gospel brings peace—peace with God, peace within, and peace with others. In the context of spiritual warfare, the shoes of the gospel of peace provide stability and confidence, enabling believers to stand firm in the truth of the gospel and to resist the enemy's attempts to disrupt their peace.

Demonic forces often seek to create turmoil, unrest, and division, leading believers to act out of fear or insecurity. However, the peace that comes from the gospel anchors believers in the assurance of God's love and faithfulness. Paul writes in Philippians 4:7, "And the peace of God, which transcends all understanding, will guard your hearts and your minds in Christ Jesus." This peace guards believers against the enemy's attempts to disturb their inner tranquility and to lead them into fear or despair.

The shoes of the gospel of peace also empower believers to proclaim the gospel to others. As they share the good news of Jesus Christ, they advance God's kingdom and push back the forces of darkness. The proclamation of the gospel is a powerful weapon in spiritual warfare, as it brings light into the darkness and sets people free from the bondage of sin and demonic oppression.

4. The Shield of Faith:

The shield of faith is designed to extinguish the flaming arrows of the evil one—arrows of doubt, fear, temptation, and accusation. In spiritual warfare, the shield of faith serves as a defense against the enemy's attempts to undermine the believer's trust in God and His promises.

Faith is not merely a mental assent to certain truths; it is a living trust in God and His character. The enemy often seeks to sow seeds of doubt, causing believers to question God's goodness, to fear the unknown, or to waver in their commitment to Him. However, the shield of faith enables believers to stand firm in their trust in God, even in the face of the enemy's attacks.

In Hebrews 11:1, faith is defined as "confidence in what we hope for and assurance about what we do not see." This confidence and assurance in God's faithfulness provide a strong defense against the enemy's attempts to instill doubt, fear, and unbelief. By taking up the shield of faith, believers are able to quench the fiery darts of the enemy and to stand firm in their faith.

5. The Helmet of Salvation:

The helmet of salvation protects the believer's mind, symbolizing the assurance of salvation in Christ. In spiritual warfare, the helmet of salvation serves as a defense against the enemy's attempts to sow seeds of doubt, fear, and confusion in the believer's mind.

The enemy often seeks to create confusion, leading believers to doubt their salvation, to question their identity in Christ, or to entertain thoughts that are contrary to God's will. However, the helmet of salvation reminds believers of their secure position in Christ and the certainty of their salvation. This assurance protects their minds and enables them to think rightly about themselves, God, and the world around them.

The helmet of salvation also empowers believers to renew their minds and to resist the sinful thoughts and attitudes that arise from the flesh and from the enemy's influence. Paul exhorts in Romans 12:2, "Do not conform to the pattern of this world, but be transformed by the renewing of your mind." This renewal of the mind, empowered by the Holy Spirit, is a crucial aspect of standing firm against the powers of darkness.

6. The Sword of the Spirit:

The sword of the Spirit is the Word of God, the only offensive weapon in the believer's armor. In spiritual warfare, the sword of the Spirit is a powerful tool for countering the enemy's lies, temptations, and attacks.

The Word of God is described as "alive and active. Sharper than any double-edged sword, it penetrates even to dividing soul and spirit, joints and marrow; it judges the thoughts and attitudes of the heart" (Hebrews 4:12). The enemy often presents temptations that appeal to the believer's desires, emotions, or circumstances. However, the Word of God provides the truth that can cut through these temptations and reveal them for what they are.

Jesus Himself demonstrated the power of the Word of God in spiritual warfare during His temptation in the wilderness (Matthew 4:1-11). Each time Satan tempted Him, Jesus responded with Scripture, effectively countering the enemy's lies and standing firm in the truth. The Word of God is a powerful weapon against demonic forces, providing believers with the wisdom and guidance needed to resist the enemy's attacks and to claim victory in Jesus' name.

7. Prayer and Dependence on the Holy Spirit:

Finally, Paul emphasizes the importance of prayer in the context of spiritual warfare: "And pray in the Spirit on all occasions with all kinds of prayers and requests. With this in mind, be alert and always keep on praying for all the Lord's people" (Ephesians 6:18). Prayer is the means by which believers maintain their connection with God and their dependence on the Holy Spirit.

In spiritual warfare, prayer is essential for seeking God's strength, guidance, and empowerment. Through prayer, believers can invite the Holy Spirit to fill them with His presence, to guide them in their decisions, and to empower them to stand firm against the powers of darkness. Prayer also serves as a way to remain vigilant and alert, recognizing the subtle tactics of the enemy and responding with spiritual discernment.

As believers pray in the Spirit, they are equipped to face the spiritual battle with confidence, knowing that they are not fighting alone but are empowered by the Holy Spirit to defeat the powers of darkness and to claim victory in Jesus' name.

Practical Steps for Defeating the Powers of Darkness

While the armor of God provides the necessary protection and resources, believers must also take practical steps to defeat the powers of darkness and to live in the victory that Christ has secured. Here are some practical steps for engaging in spiritual warfare and overcoming demonic forces:

1. Know Your Authority in Christ:

The first step in defeating the powers of darkness is to know and understand your authority in Christ. This authority is not based on your own strength or merit but on the victory that Jesus Christ has already won. Believers have been given authority over demonic forces through their union with Christ, and this authority is exercised in His name.

It is important to remind yourself regularly of this truth and to stand firm in your identity as a child of God. Knowing your authority in Christ gives you the confidence to resist the enemy and to claim victory in Jesus' name.

2. Engage in Regular Prayer and Fasting:

Prayer is a powerful weapon in spiritual warfare, and regular, intentional prayer is essential for maintaining your spiritual strength and connection with God. In addition to personal prayer, consider incorporating fasting into your spiritual discipline. Fasting is a way to deny the flesh and to focus more intently on God, seeking His guidance, strength, and protection in spiritual warfare.

Jesus emphasized the importance of prayer and fasting in spiritual warfare, particularly in cases of demonic oppression. In Matthew 17:21, after casting out a demon that the disciples were unable to expel, Jesus said, "However, this kind does not go out except by prayer and fasting." This statement underscores the power of prayer and fasting in defeating the powers of darkness.

3. Immerse Yourself in God's Word:

Immersing yourself in Scripture is crucial for defeating the powers of darkness. The Word of God provides the truth and wisdom needed to counter the enemy's lies and temptations. Regular reading, studying, and meditating on Scripture helps to renew your mind and to align your thoughts and attitudes with God's will.

Memorizing key verses that address specific areas of struggle can also be a powerful tool in spiritual warfare. When faced with temptation or attack, you can recall and declare these scriptures, using the sword of the Spirit to combat the enemy's influence.

4. Cultivate a Life of Worship and Praise:

Worship and praise are powerful weapons in spiritual warfare. When you worship God, you declare His greatness, power, and authority over all things, including the powers of darkness. Worship shifts your focus from the enemy's attacks to the greatness of God, reminding you of His sovereignty and faithfulness.

In the Bible, we see several examples of the power of worship in spiritual warfare. One such example is the story of King Jehoshaphat in 2 Chronicles 20. When faced with a vast army, Jehoshaphat led the people in worship, and God miraculously delivered them from their enemies. As you cultivate a life of worship and praise, you create an atmosphere where the presence of God is manifested, and the enemy's influence is diminished.

5. Stay Connected to the Body of Christ:

Defeating the powers of darkness is not something you can do in isolation; it requires the support and encouragement of other believers. Staying connected to the Body of Christ—through regular fellowship, worship, and accountability—is essential for maintaining spiritual strength and for resisting the enemy's attacks.

Engaging in small groups, discipleship relationships, or accountability partnerships provides a safe space to share your struggles, to receive prayer and encouragement, and to hold one another accountable in your walk with God.

6. Be Vigilant and Discern the Enemy's Tactics:

Vigilance and discernment are crucial in spiritual warfare. The enemy often operates subtly, seeking to deceive, distract, or discourage believers. By staying vigilant and discerning the enemy's tactics, you can recognize his schemes and respond with spiritual wisdom and authority.

Jesus warned His disciples to be watchful and alert in the face of spiritual opposition (Mark 13:33). This vigilance involves being aware of the enemy's strategies, guarding your heart and mind, and staying rooted in the truth of God's Word.

Proclaim the Victory of Jesus Christ:

Finally, proclaim the victory of Jesus Christ over the powers of darkness. The enemy's defeat was secured through the cross and resurrection of Jesus, and this victory is the foundation of your authority in spiritual warfare. By proclaiming this victory in prayer, worship, and daily life, you assert the authority of Christ over the enemy and declare His lordship in every area of your life.

Revelation 12:11 declares, "They triumphed over him by the blood of the Lamb and by the word of their testimony; they did not love their lives so much as to shrink from death." This testimony of victory is a powerful weapon in spiritual warfare, reminding both you and the enemy of the authority and power of Jesus Christ.

Conclusion: Standing Firm in Victory Over the Powers of Darkness

The battle against the powers of darkness is a significant aspect of spiritual warfare, requiring vigilance, discernment, and reliance on the power and authority of Jesus Christ. While demonic forces are powerful and malevolent, believers are not left to fight this battle alone. Through the victory of Jesus Christ, believers have been given authority over these forces and are equipped with the armor of God to stand firm and to claim victory in His name.

The armor of God, as described in Ephesians 6:10-18, provides the necessary protection and resources for defeating the powers of darkness. Each piece of armor equips believers with the truth, righteousness, peace, faith, salvation, and the Word of God—essential tools for standing firm against the enemy and for advancing God's kingdom.

As believers take practical steps to engage in spiritual warfare—through prayer, fasting, immersion in God's Word, worship, fellowship, vigilance, and the proclamation of Christ's victory—they experience the power and authority of Jesus Christ at work in their lives. These steps are not merely defensive but are offensive strategies that push back the forces of darkness and bring light into the world.

In the words of the Apostle Paul, "Finally, be strong in the Lord and in his mighty power. Put on the full armor of God, so that you can take your stand against the devil's schemes" (Ephesians 6:10-11). This is the call to every believer—to be strong in the Lord, to stand firm in His power, and to defeat the powers of darkness through the victory of Jesus Christ. As we do so, we reflect the light of Christ, bring glory to God, and advance His kingdom in the world.

Chapter 14: The Assurance of Victory

Theme: Confidence in Christ's ultimate victory.

Reflection: Discuss the assurance that, through Christ, believers already have victory in spiritual warfare. Reflect on the hope and confidence this brings, and how it empowers us to face challenges with courage.

The journey of faith is often marked by challenges, battles, and struggles, both seen and unseen. As believers, we are engaged in a spiritual warfare that is intense and unrelenting. Yet, amid the conflict, there is a profound and unshakable truth that provides hope, strength, and courage: through Jesus Christ, we already have victory. This assurance of victory is not a distant hope or a vague possibility; it is a present reality grounded in the finished work of Christ. Understanding and embracing this truth transforms the way we face spiritual battles and empowers us to live with confidence, courage, and unwavering hope.

In this chapter, we will explore the assurance of victory that believers have in Christ, examining the scriptural foundations for this confidence. We will reflect on how this assurance shapes our approach to spiritual warfare, enabling us to face challenges with courage and to live in the victory that Christ has secured. Through these reflections, we will gain a deeper understanding of the power and hope that comes from knowing that, in Christ, we are more than conquerors.

The Foundation of Our Victory: The Work of Christ

The assurance of victory in spiritual warfare is not based on our own strength, wisdom, or efforts. It is rooted entirely in the person and work of Jesus Christ. Through His life, death, resurrection, and ascension, Christ has secured victory over sin, death, and the powers of darkness. This victory is complete, irrevocable, and available to all who trust in Him.

1. The Victory of the Cross:

At the heart of the Christian faith is the cross of Jesus Christ. The cross is not merely a symbol of suffering and sacrifice; it is the decisive battlefield where the forces of sin, death, and Satan were defeated. In Colossians 2:13-15, Paul writes, "When you were dead in your sins and in the uncircumcision of your flesh, God made you alive with Christ. He forgave us all our sins, having canceled the charge of our legal indebtedness, which stood against us and condemned us; he has taken it away, nailing it to the cross. And having disarmed the powers and authorities, he made a public spectacle of them, triumphing over them by the cross."

This passage reveals the comprehensive nature of Christ's victory on the cross. Through His sacrificial death, Jesus dealt with the problem of sin, canceling the debt that stood against us and removing the condemnation that we deserved. But His victory did not end there; He also disarmed the powers and authorities—demonic forces that oppose God and His people. By triumphing over them on the cross, Jesus made a public spectacle of them, declaring His supremacy and authority.

The cross, therefore, is the foundation of our victory in spiritual warfare. It is the place where the power of sin was broken, the accusations of the enemy were silenced, and the dominion of darkness was shattered. When we stand in the victory of the cross, we stand in the power of Christ's finished work, confident that the enemy has been defeated and that we are free from his power.

2. The Power of the Resurrection:

The victory of the cross is inseparably linked to the victory of the resurrection. If the cross was the battlefield, the resurrection was the declaration of victory. When Jesus rose from the dead, He conquered the power of death and demonstrated His authority over all things. In 1 Corinthians 15:54-57, Paul exults in the victory of the resurrection: "When the perishable has been clothed with the imperishable, and the mortal with immortality, then the saying that is written will come true: 'Death has been swallowed up in victory.' 'Where, O death, is your victory? Where, O death, is your sting?' The sting of death is sin, and the power of sin is the law. But thanks be to God! He gives us the victory through our Lord Jesus Christ."

The resurrection is the ultimate proof that Jesus has defeated death and that His victory is complete. For believers, the resurrection is not just a historical event; it is the source of our hope and the guarantee of our own resurrection.

Because Jesus lives, we too shall live, and the power of death has no hold over us.

This resurrection power is also at work in us through the Holy Spirit. Paul writes in Romans 8:11, "And if the Spirit of him who raised Jesus from the dead is living in you, he who raised Christ from the dead will also give life to your mortal bodies because of his Spirit who lives in you." The same power that raised Jesus from the dead is alive and active in us, empowering us to live in victory over sin, death, and the powers of darkness.

3. The Authority of the Ascended Christ:

After His resurrection, Jesus ascended into heaven and was exalted to the right hand of the Father. This exaltation signifies His authority and lordship over all creation. In Ephesians 1:19-23, Paul prays that believers would understand "his incomparably great power for us who believe. That power is the same as the mighty strength he exerted when he raised Christ from the dead and seated him at his right hand in the heavenly realms, far above all rule and authority, power and dominion, and every name that is invoked, not only in the present age but also in the one to come. And God placed all things under his feet and appointed him to be head over everything for the church, which is his body, the fullness of him who fills everything in every way."

The ascension and exaltation of Christ mean that He reigns as the sovereign Lord over all things. Every power, authority, and dominion is subject to Him, and He exercises His rule for the benefit of His church. This truth is the basis of our confidence in spiritual warfare. No matter what forces we face, we can be assured that Christ is greater, and His authority is supreme.

Because we are united with Christ, we share in His authority. Paul writes in Ephesians 2:6, "And God raised us up with Christ and seated us with him in the heavenly realms in Christ Jesus." This means that, spiritually speaking, we are seated with Christ in a position of authority. We are not fighting for victory; we are fighting from victory, secure in the authority of the ascended Christ.

Living in the Assurance of Victory

Understanding the foundation of our victory in Christ is essential, but it is also important to know how to live in that victory daily. The assurance of victory is not just a theological concept; it is a practical reality that empowers us to face challenges with courage and to live with hope and confidence. Here are some key aspects of living in the assurance of victory:

1. Confidence in Christ's Finished Work:

The assurance of victory begins with confidence in Christ's finished work. This confidence is not based on our own abilities, righteousness, or achievements; it is rooted entirely in what Jesus has done on our behalf. When we understand that Christ's victory is complete and that we share in that victory through faith, we can approach spiritual warfare with boldness and courage.

This confidence is reflected in the words of Paul in Romans 8:31-34: "What, then, shall we say in response to these things? If God is for us, who can be against us? He who did not spare his own Son, but gave him up for us all—how will he not also, along with him, graciously give us all things? Who will bring any charge against those whom God has chosen? It is God who justifies. Who then is the one who condemns? No one. Christ Jesus who died—more than that, who was raised to life—is at the right hand of God and is also interceding for us."

Paul's confidence is based on the unassailable truth that Christ has died, been raised, and is now interceding for us at the right hand of God. Because of this, no accusation, condemnation, or opposition can stand against us. We are secure in Christ, and our victory is assured.

2. The Power of the Holy Spirit:

Living in the assurance of victory also involves relying on the power of the Holy Spirit. The Holy Spirit is the one who applies the victory of Christ to our lives, empowering us to resist temptation, overcome sin, and stand firm against the enemy. The Spirit's presence within us is the guarantee of our victory, and His power enables us to live out that victory in our daily lives.

In Romans 8:37, Paul declares, "No, in all these things we are more than conquerors through him who loved us." The phrase "more than conquerors" speaks of overwhelming victory—victory that is not just sufficient but abundant. This victory is made possible through the power of the Holy Spirit, who enables us to rise above every challenge and to walk in the triumph that Christ has secured.

The Holy Spirit also provides us with discernment, wisdom, and guidance in the midst of spiritual warfare. As we walk in the Spirit, we are able to recognize the enemy's tactics, to respond with the truth of God's Word, and to stand firm in our identity as victorious children of God.

3. Standing Firm in Faith:

The assurance of victory is not a passive confidence; it is an active stance that requires us to stand firm in faith. Throughout Scripture, believers are exhorted to stand firm in the face of opposition, to hold fast to their confession of faith, and to resist the devil. This standing firm is not done in our own strength but in the strength of the Lord and the power of His might.

In Ephesians 6:10-13, Paul writes, "Finally, be strong in the Lord and in his mighty power. Put on the full armor of God, so that you can take your stand against the devil's schemes. For our struggle is not against flesh and blood, but against the rulers, against the authorities, against the powers of this dark world and against the spiritual forces of evil in the heavenly realms. Therefore put on the full armor of God, so that when the day of evil comes, you may be able to stand your ground, and after you have done everything, to stand."

The call to stand firm is a call to perseverance and endurance. It is a recognition that the battle is real, but so is the victory. As we put on the full armor of God and stand firm in faith, we are able to resist the enemy and to claim the victory that is already ours in Christ.

4. Living with Courage and Hope:

The assurance of victory empowers us to live with courage and hope, even in the face of adversity. Courage is not the absence of fear; it is the confidence to move forward despite fear, knowing that God is with us and that victory is assured. Hope is not wishful thinking; it is the confident expectation of good because of God's promises and faithfulness.

In Joshua 1:9, God exhorted Joshua as he prepared to lead the Israelites into the Promised Land: "Have I not commanded you? Be strong and courageous. Do not be afraid; do not be discouraged, for the Lord your God will be with you wherever you go." This command to be strong and courageous is grounded in the assurance of God's presence and His promise of victory.

As believers, we are called to live with the same courage and hope. No matter what challenges we face—whether spiritual, emotional, or physical—we can be confident that God is with us and that His victory is certain. This confidence allows us to face every challenge with a spirit of boldness, knowing that we are not alone and that the outcome is secure.

5. Overcoming by the Word of Our Testimony:

The assurance of victory is also expressed through the word of our testimony. In Revelation 12:11, we are told, "They triumphed over him by the blood of the Lamb and by the word of their testimony; they did not love their lives so much as to shrink from death." The word of our testimony is a powerful weapon in spiritual warfare, as it declares the truth of what Christ has done in our lives and proclaims His victory over the enemy.

Sharing our testimony is not just about recounting past victories; it is about affirming our ongoing confidence in Christ's victory and standing firm in that truth. When we declare what God has done, we remind ourselves and others of His faithfulness, and we reinforce our faith in His power to overcome any obstacle.

The word of our testimony also serves as a witness to the world. As we live out our victory in Christ and share our stories of His faithfulness, we bear witness to the reality of His power and the hope that is available to all who trust in Him. Our testimony is a light that shines in the darkness, pointing others to the source of our victory—Jesus Christ.

6. Resting in God's Sovereignty:

Finally, living in the assurance of victory involves resting in God's sovereignty. God's sovereignty means that He is in control of all things, that nothing happens outside of His will or His knowledge, and that He is working all things together for the good of those who love Him and are called according to His purpose (Romans 8:28).

Resting in God's sovereignty allows us to trust Him completely, even when circumstances are difficult or when the outcome is uncertain. It means believing that God is at work, even in the midst of our trials, and that His plans for us are good. This trust in God's sovereignty provides a deep sense of peace and security, knowing that we are held in His hands and that His purposes will prevail.

In Isaiah 46:9-10, God declares, "I am God, and there is no other; I am God, and there is none like me. I make known the end from the beginning, from ancient times, what is still to come. I say, 'My purpose will stand, and I will do all that I please.'" This declaration of God's sovereignty is a powerful reminder that our victory is secure because it is part of His unchanging purpose and plan.

The Hope of Ultimate Victory

While we experience victory in Christ in our daily lives, there is also a future aspect to our victory—a hope of ultimate victory that will be fully realized at the return of Christ. This ultimate victory includes the final defeat of all evil, the establishment of God's kingdom in its fullness, and the consummation of all things in Christ. This hope is a source of great encouragement and strength as we navigate the challenges of life.

1. The Return of Christ:

The return of Christ is the culmination of God's redemptive plan and the moment when ultimate victory will be fully realized. Jesus Himself spoke of His return, promising that He would come again to judge the living and the dead, to establish His kingdom, and to make all things new. In Matthew 24:30-31, Jesus describes His return: "Then will appear the sign of the Son of Man in heaven. And then all the peoples of the earth will mourn when they see the Son of Man coming on the clouds of heaven, with power and great glory. And he will send his angels with a loud trumpet call, and they will gather his elect from the four winds, from one end of the heavens to the other."

The return of Christ is a moment of ultimate victory, when every knee will bow and every tongue will confess that Jesus Christ is Lord (Philippians 2:10-11). For believers, this is a moment of great joy and hope, as we will be united with Christ forever and will share in His glory.

The hope of Christ's return provides perspective and encouragement in the midst of our present struggles. It reminds us that our current battles are temporary and that a day is coming when all things will be made right. This hope empowers us to persevere, knowing that ultimate victory is assured.

2. The Defeat of All Evil:

The return of Christ also signals the final defeat of all evil. Satan, who has been a defeated foe since the cross, will be utterly vanquished and cast into the lake of fire, along with all who have followed him (Revelation 20:10). The powers of darkness that have opposed God's people will be destroyed, and there will be no more sin, suffering, or death.

Revelation 21:4-5 describes this moment of ultimate victory: "He will wipe every tear from their eyes. There will be no more death or mourning or crying or pain, for the old order of things has passed away. He who was seated on the throne said, 'I am making everything new!'"

The final defeat of evil means that believers will live in a new heaven and a new earth, where righteousness dwells and where we will experience the fullness of God's presence and glory. This promise of ultimate victory over evil gives us hope and courage to face the challenges of this present age, knowing that evil will not have the last word.

3. The Consummation of All Things in Christ:

The ultimate victory also includes the consummation of all things in Christ. This means that everything in creation will be brought into perfect harmony under the lordship of Jesus Christ. In Ephesians 1:9-10, Paul writes about God's plan "to bring unity to all things in heaven and on earth under Christ."

This consummation involves the restoration of all that was broken by sin, the renewal of creation, and the fulfillment of God's purposes for His people. We will reign with Christ, sharing in His glory and participating in His eternal kingdom.

The hope of this ultimate victory gives us a sense of purpose and destiny. It reminds us that our lives are part of a much larger story—God's story of redemption and restoration. As we live in the assurance of victory, we do so with the expectation that the best is yet to come, that God's kingdom will come in its fullness, and that we will share in the joy of His eternal reign.

Conclusion: Living in the Light of Victory

The assurance of victory in Christ is a powerful and transformative truth that shapes every aspect of our lives. It is the foundation of our confidence, the source of our courage, and the basis of our hope. Through the finished work of Jesus Christ—His life, death, resurrection, and ascension—believers are already victorious, and this victory is both a present reality and a future hope.

As we live in the light of this victory, we are called to stand firm in faith, to walk in the power of the Holy Spirit, and to face every challenge with courage and hope. We are not fighting for victory; we are fighting from victory, secure in the knowledge that the battle has already been won. This assurance empowers us to overcome the powers of darkness, to resist the enemy's schemes, and to live in the freedom and joy that Christ has purchased for us.

Moreover, the hope of ultimate victory—Christ's return, the defeat of all evil, and the consummation of all things in Him—gives us perspective and strength as we navigate the trials and tribulations of this life. We know that our struggles are temporary and that a glorious future awaits us, where we will share in Christ's victory and reign with Him forever.

In the words of the Apostle Paul, "Thanks be to God! He gives us the victory through our Lord Jesus Christ" (1 Corinthians 15:57). This is the declaration of every believer—one of gratitude, confidence, and unshakable hope. As we live in the assurance of victory, we bring glory to God, bear witness to the power of the Gospel, and reflect the light of Christ to a world in need.

Chapter 15: Living as a Spiritual Warrior

Theme: Applying the armor of God in daily life.

Reflection: Conclude with practical ways to live as a spiritual warrior in everyday life. Reflect on how to continuously put on the full armor of God and maintain a lifestyle that reflects readiness for spiritual warfare.

As we come to the conclusion of this exploration into spiritual warfare and the armor of God, it is essential to recognize that the concepts and principles we have discussed are not merely theoretical or reserved for moments of crisis. Instead, they are meant to be lived out in the daily realities of life, guiding our thoughts, actions, and decisions. Living as a spiritual warrior is about embodying a lifestyle that is grounded in the truth of God's Word, empowered by the Holy Spirit, and marked by a constant readiness for the battles that come our way.

In this final chapter, we will explore practical ways to live as a spiritual warrior in everyday life. We will reflect on how to continuously put on the full armor of God and how to maintain a lifestyle that is prepared for spiritual warfare. By integrating these principles into our daily lives, we can walk in the victory that Christ has secured for us and reflect His light in a world that is often dark and challenging.

The Call to Live as a Spiritual Warrior

The call to live as a spiritual warrior is not a special assignment for a select few; it is a call that is extended to every believer. In Ephesians 6:10-18, the Apostle Paul exhorts all believers to "put on the full armor of God" so that they may "take their stand against the devil's schemes" and "stand firm" in the face of spiritual opposition. This passage is a rallying cry for the church, reminding us that we are engaged in a spiritual battle that requires vigilance, discipline, and dependence on God.

The imagery of a warrior clad in armor is a powerful metaphor for the Christian life. Just as a soldier prepares for battle by putting on physical armor, we are called to prepare for the spiritual battles we face by putting on the spiritual armor that God provides. This armor is not optional; it is essential for living a victorious Christian life. Without it, we are vulnerable to the enemy's attacks and ill-equipped to stand firm in our faith.

Living as a spiritual warrior means recognizing the reality of spiritual warfare and choosing to be proactive in our approach to the Christian life. It involves a commitment to spiritual disciplines, a reliance on the Holy Spirit, and a willingness to engage in the battle with courage and confidence. It is about living with a sense of purpose and readiness, knowing that we are called to stand firm in the faith and to advance God's kingdom in the world.

Continuously Putting on the Full Armor of God

One of the key aspects of living as a spiritual warrior is the continuous act of putting on the full armor of God. This is not a one-time event but a daily practice that requires intentionality and discipline. Each piece of the armor represents a critical aspect of our spiritual defense and offense, and together they provide comprehensive protection against the enemy's schemes.

1. The Belt of Truth:

The belt of truth is the first piece of armor mentioned by Paul, and it represents the foundational truth of God's Word. Putting on the belt of truth involves a commitment to living in the light of God's truth, both in our beliefs and in our actions. It means rejecting the lies and deceptions of the enemy and standing firm in the truth of who God is and who we are in Christ.

To continuously put on the belt of truth, we must immerse ourselves in Scripture, allowing God's Word to shape our thinking, our values, and our decisions. This involves regular Bible study, meditation on Scripture, and the application of biblical principles to our daily lives. The more we internalize God's truth, the more equipped we are to recognize and reject the lies of the enemy.

In practical terms, putting on the belt of truth might involve starting each day with a time of prayer and Bible reading, setting the tone for the day with a focus on God's truth. It could also mean memorizing key verses that address specific areas of struggle, so that when the enemy attacks with lies or temptations, we can respond with the truth of God's Word.

2. The Breastplate of Righteousness:

The breastplate of righteousness protects the believer's heart, symbolizing the righteousness that comes from God and is imputed to us through faith in Christ. To continuously put on the breastplate of righteousness, we must live in the reality of our justification by faith, recognizing that our righteousness is not based on our own performance but on the finished work of Christ.

This involves rejecting the enemy's accusations and standing firm in the knowledge that we are clothed in the righteousness of Christ. It also means pursuing practical righteousness in our daily lives, striving to live in a way that reflects our identity as children of God. This might involve making intentional choices to avoid situations that could lead to sin, cultivating habits of holiness, and seeking accountability in areas of weakness.

In practical terms, putting on the breastplate of righteousness might involve daily confessing any known sin to God, receiving His forgiveness, and asking for the Holy Spirit's strength to live in obedience. It could also mean seeking out relationships with other believers who can encourage and support us in our pursuit of righteousness.

3. The Shoes of the Gospel of Peace:

The shoes of the gospel of peace equip us to stand firm and to move forward in our spiritual walk. To continuously put on these shoes, we must ground ourselves in the peace that comes from the gospel, allowing it to anchor us in the midst of life's challenges and to motivate us to share that peace with others.

This involves cultivating a deep sense of peace with God, peace within ourselves, and peace with others. It also means being ready to share the gospel with those who do not yet know Christ, bringing the message of peace to a world in need. In practical terms, this might involve taking time each day to reflect on the gospel and to thank God for the peace that it brings. It could also mean being intentional about seeking reconciliation in relationships where there is conflict and being open to opportunities to share the gospel with others.

Additionally, putting on the shoes of the gospel of peace might involve praying for opportunities to be a peacemaker in our communities, whether that means standing up for justice, offering forgiveness, or simply being a calming presence in a stressful situation.

4. The Shield of Faith:

The shield of faith is designed to extinguish the flaming arrows of the evil one—arrows of doubt, fear, temptation, and accusation. To continuously take up the shield of faith, we must actively trust in God's promises and character, even when circumstances are difficult or the enemy's attacks are intense.

This involves choosing to believe God's Word over our feelings, our circumstances, and the lies of the enemy. It means cultivating a deep and abiding faith in God's goodness, His faithfulness, and His ability to deliver us from every attack. In practical terms, this might involve developing a habit of praying Scripture, using God's promises as a shield against the enemy's attacks. It could also mean surrounding ourselves with other believers who can encourage our faith and stand with us in times of trial.

Putting on the shield of faith might also involve taking steps of faith in our daily lives, trusting God to lead us, provide for us, and protect us as we walk in obedience to His will. This could mean stepping out of our comfort zones to serve others, to share the gospel, or to pursue a calling that God has placed on our hearts.

5. The Helmet of Salvation:

The helmet of salvation protects the believer's mind, symbolizing the assurance of salvation in Christ. To continuously put on the helmet of salvation, we must guard our minds against the enemy's attempts to sow seeds of doubt, fear, and confusion.

This involves focusing our thoughts on the truth of our salvation, meditating on the security we have in Christ, and rejecting any thoughts that are contrary to God's Word. It also means renewing our minds through the study of Scripture, allowing the Holy Spirit to transform our thinking and align it with God's will. In practical terms, this might involve setting aside time each day to reflect on the gospel and to thank God for the gift of salvation. It could also mean being intentional about what we allow into our minds, choosing to fill our thoughts with things that are true, noble, right, pure, lovely, and admirable (Philippians 4:8).

Putting on the helmet of salvation might also involve developing a habit of taking every thought captive to the obedience of Christ (2 Corinthians 10:5), challenging any thoughts that lead to doubt, fear, or confusion, and replacing them with the truth of God's Word.

6. The Sword of the Spirit:

The sword of the Spirit is the Word of God, the only offensive weapon in the believer's armor. To continuously take up the sword of the Spirit, we must be diligent in studying, meditating on, and applying Scripture to our lives.

This involves developing a deep love for God's Word, allowing it to shape our beliefs, our values, and our actions. It also means being ready to use Scripture in the midst of spiritual warfare, responding to the enemy's attacks with the truth of God's Word. In practical terms, this might involve memorizing key verses that address specific areas of struggle, so that when the enemy attacks, we can respond with the truth of Scripture. It could also mean regularly studying the Bible in a systematic way, seeking to understand its meaning and apply its teachings to our lives.

Putting on the sword of the Spirit might also involve using Scripture in our prayers, praying God's promises over our lives and the lives of others, and declaring His truth in the face of the enemy's lies.

7. Prayer and Vigilance:

Finally, Paul emphasizes the importance of prayer in the context of spiritual warfare: "And pray in the Spirit on all occasions with all kinds of prayers and requests. With this in mind, be alert and always keep on praying for all the Lord's people" (Ephesians 6:18). Prayer is the means by which we maintain our connection with God and our dependence on the Holy Spirit.

To continuously put on the full armor of God, we must cultivate a lifestyle of prayer and vigilance. This involves being intentional about setting aside time each day for prayer, seeking God's guidance, strength, and protection. It also means remaining vigilant and alert, recognizing the subtle tactics of the enemy and responding with spiritual discernment.

In practical terms, this might involve developing a daily prayer routine that includes praise, confession, thanksgiving, and supplication. It could also mean being intentional about praying for others, interceding on behalf of fellow believers who are facing spiritual battles.

Additionally, living as a spiritual warrior involves maintaining a sense of vigilance throughout the day, being aware of the spiritual dynamics at play in our lives and the lives of those around us. This might involve regularly examining our hearts and minds, asking God to reveal any areas of vulnerability or compromise, and taking steps to address them.

Maintaining a Lifestyle of Readiness for Spiritual Warfare

Living as a spiritual warrior requires more than just putting on the armor of God; it requires maintaining a lifestyle that reflects readiness for spiritual warfare. This involves cultivating spiritual disciplines, building strong relationships with other believers, and remaining rooted in the truth of God's Word.

1. Cultivating Spiritual Disciplines:

Spiritual disciplines are the practices that help us grow in our relationship with God and prepare us for spiritual warfare. These disciplines include prayer, Bible study, fasting, worship, and solitude, among others. By cultivating these disciplines, we strengthen our spiritual muscles and develop the habits that sustain us in the battle.

In practical terms, cultivating spiritual disciplines might involve setting aside specific times each day for prayer and Bible study, committing to regular times of fasting and solitude, and making worship a central part of our lives. It could also mean being intentional about participating in corporate worship and fellowship, recognizing the importance of gathering with other believers for encouragement and accountability.

Spiritual disciplines are not an end in themselves; they are the means by which we draw closer to God and become more like Christ. As we cultivate these disciplines, we become more attuned to the Holy Spirit's leading, more grounded in God's truth, and more equipped to stand firm in the face of spiritual opposition.

2. Building Strong Relationships with Other Believers:

One of the most important aspects of living as a spiritual warrior is building strong relationships with other believers. Spiritual warfare is not something we are meant to face alone; we need the support, encouragement, and accountability of other members of the body of Christ.

In practical terms, building strong relationships might involve joining a small group or Bible study, finding a prayer partner or accountability partner, and being intentional about investing in relationships with other believers. It could also mean being open and honest about our struggles, allowing others to speak into our lives and to walk alongside us in the battle.

The Bible emphasizes the importance of community in the Christian life. In Hebrews 10:24-25, we are exhorted, "And let us consider how we may spur one another on toward love and good deeds, not giving up meeting together, as some are in the habit of doing, but encouraging one another—and all the more as you see the Day approaching." By building strong relationships with other believers, we create a support system that helps us to stay strong in the faith and to persevere in the face of spiritual warfare.

3. Remaining Rooted in the Truth of God's Word:

To live as a spiritual warrior, we must remain rooted in the truth of God's Word. The enemy's primary tactic is deception, and the only way to counter his lies is with the truth of Scripture. By staying grounded in God's Word, we ensure that our beliefs, values, and decisions are aligned with His will and that we are equipped to stand firm in the battle.

In practical terms, remaining rooted in the truth might involve committing to a regular Bible reading plan, studying Scripture in depth, and seeking to apply its teachings to our daily lives. It could also mean being intentional about listening to sound biblical teaching, whether through sermons, podcasts, or books, and being discerning about the messages we allow into our minds.

The psalmist declares in Psalm 119:105, "Your word is a lamp for my feet, a light on my path." By remaining rooted in God's Word, we ensure that our path is illuminated by His truth and that we are guided by His wisdom in all that we do.

4. Practicing Spiritual Vigilance:

Spiritual vigilance is the practice of staying alert and aware of the spiritual dynamics at play in our lives. It involves being mindful of the enemy's tactics, recognizing areas of vulnerability, and taking proactive steps to guard against spiritual attack.

In practical terms, practicing spiritual vigilance might involve regularly examining our hearts and minds, asking God to reveal any areas of compromise or vulnerability. It could also mean being intentional about setting boundaries in our lives, avoiding situations or relationships that could lead to sin or spiritual defeat.

Jesus warned His disciples to "watch and pray so that you will not fall into temptation" (Matthew 26:41). By practicing spiritual vigilance, we ensure that we are prepared for the battles that come our way and that we are able to stand firm in the face of spiritual opposition.

5. Living with a Sense of Purpose and Mission:

Finally, living as a spiritual warrior involves living with a sense of purpose and mission. We are not called to simply survive the battle; we are called to advance God's kingdom in the world. This means living with intentionality, recognizing that our lives have eternal significance and that we have been given a mission to fulfill.

In practical terms, living with a sense of purpose and mission might involve seeking God's guidance for how He wants to use us in our families, communities, and workplaces. It could mean being intentional about sharing the gospel with others, serving those in need, and standing up for justice and righteousness.

The Apostle Paul encourages us to "run with perseverance the race marked out for us, fixing our eyes on Jesus, the pioneer and perfecter of faith" (Hebrews 12:1-2). By living with a sense of purpose and mission, we ensure that our lives are aligned with God's will and that we are making a lasting impact for His kingdom.

Conclusion: Embracing the Identity of a Spiritual Warrior

As we conclude this exploration of spiritual warfare and the armor of God, it is important to recognize that living as a spiritual warrior is not just about what we do; it is about who we are. It is about embracing our identity as children of God, called to stand firm in the faith and to advance His kingdom in the world. It is about living with a sense of readiness, purpose, and mission, knowing that we are engaged in a spiritual battle that has eternal significance.

Living as a spiritual warrior requires continuous effort and intentionality. It involves putting on the full armor of God every day, cultivating spiritual disciplines, building strong relationships with other believers, remaining rooted in the truth of God's Word, and practicing spiritual vigilance. It also involves living with a sense of purpose and mission, recognizing that our lives have been entrusted with a divine calling.

As we embrace this identity and live out these principles, we can be confident that we are not fighting alone. We are empowered by the Holy Spirit, guided by God's Word, and supported by the body of Christ. We are more than conquerors through Him who loved us (Romans 8:37), and we can face every challenge with courage and hope, knowing that the victory is already ours in Christ.

In the words of the Apostle Paul, "Be on your guard; stand firm in the faith; be courageous; be strong. Do everything in love" (1 Corinthians 16:13-14). This is the call to every believer—to live as a spiritual warrior, to stand firm in the faith, and to reflect the love of Christ in all that we do. As we do so, we bring glory to God, advance His kingdom, and fulfill the mission that He has entrusted to us.

Don't miss out!

Visit the website below and you can sign up to receive emails whenever Gregory Allen Parker publishes a new book. There's no charge and no obligation.

https://books2read.com/r/B-A-SLYZB-YXYVE

BOOKS 2 READ

Connecting independent readers to independent writers.

Did you love *The Armor of God*? Then you should read *Light in the Darkness*[1] by Gregory Allen Parker!

[2]

Light in the Darkness is a compelling journey through 15 theological reflections that illuminate the profound significance of light in the Bible. From the creation of light to the promise of eternal light in God's presence, this Christian Biblical fiction explores how God's light guides, redeems, and sustains believers. Each chapter delves into a different aspect of light, offering insights into faith, hope, and the ultimate victory over darkness. Perfect for readers seeking spiritual depth and a deeper understanding of God's redemptive plan through the lens of His eternal light.

---

1. https://books2read.com/u/4EgvZo

2. https://books2read.com/u/4EgvZo

About the Author

Pastor Gregory Allen Parker, a graduate of Trinity Theological Seminary, is a devoted pastor and acclaimed author of Christian fiction. With over two decades of ministry experience, his books explore faith's challenges and triumphs, offering readers inspiring and spiritually rich narratives. Celebrated for his compassionate pastoral care and insightful sermons, Pastor Parker's storytelling reflects his deep understanding of Christian values. When not writing or preaching, he enjoys family time, community volunteering, and the outdoors, continuing to inspire and uplift through his faith and craft.